THE DANVILLE STAGECOACH ROBBERY

Riding on the Danville stagecoach as a young lad, Jason Colebrook survived a robbery but was badly wounded. Twenty years later, determined to uncover the truth, he gets a lead to a frontier town in Nebraska where he falls foul of a local gang, but also falls for a beautiful redhead — only to discover she is entangled in a network of corruption. Although help arrives unexpectedly from the local hotel owner's daughter, Jason has to use all his cunning, determination and gun skills to see that justice is done.

FRANK CHANDLER

THE DANVILLE STAGECOACH ROBBERY

Complete and Unabridged

LINFORD
Leicester

First published in Great Britain in 2016 by
Robert Hale
an imprint of The Crowood Press
Wiltshire

First Linford Edition
published 2018
by arrangement with
The Crowood Press
Wiltshire

A catalogue record for this book is available
from the British Library.

ISBN 978–1–4448–3914–2

Published by
F. A. Thorpe (Publishing)
Anstey, Leicestershire

Set by Words & Graphics Ltd.
Anstey, Leicestershire
Printed and bound in Great Britain by
T. J. International Ltd., Padstow, Cornwall

This book is printed on acid-free paper

1

With a shuddering sigh the train slid to a halt in the busy cattle town of Filmont Junction on the western edge of Nebraska territory. There was a loud hissing of steam and clanking of bells. Jason Colebrook was quickly out of his seat; he grabbed his saddle-bags and made his way to the end of the carriage. His progress was suddenly arrested by an elderly lady whose frail appearance did not match her steely grey eyes, which she fixed on him.

'Young man, could you reach my valise?' she asked, pointing to the carpet bag in the overhead rack.

'Certainly, ma'am,' he replied courteously, easing the bag to the floor. 'Shall I carry it outside?'

'That would be kind.'

Jason put the bag down beside the lady as she arranged her hat, fixing it with a long jewelled pin. 'My pleasure, ma'am.'

'Thank you,' she said with a wide smile, pressing a silver dollar into his hand.

'Oh, that won't be necessary,' he said.

'No, not necessary but it is a gift and you shouldn't refuse a gift.'

Jason touched his hat, smiled at the old lady and slipped the dollar into his shirt pocket while collecting his mount from the freight car. Leading his fine skewbald quarter horse to the street, he scanned for the saloon and was soon ordering a beer from the barkeep. He licked his lips in anticipation as the amber liquid was poured into a glass. The train ride had been too long, too hot and his throat was too dry. Three days and 600 miles were now behind him. He put his hand into his shirt pocket to pay with the lady's silver dollar, but let it drop back. It was a gift; you don't part with gifts.

He put the glass to his lips and began a long gulp but was unexpectedly interrupted by an ill-phrased question. Jason hadn't noticed the cattleman standing just along the bar and was slightly taken aback when the man turned to him and said, 'Looking for work, son?'

Having just had his twenty-eighth birthday before setting out on this journey, Jason had a very strong aversion to being called 'son'. He turned to the man who had moved nearer and took a long hard look at him. In his fifties, with greying hair at the temples, a sun-wrinkled face, muscled arms, calloused fingers and rough hands, he was almost certainly a cattleman. Jason dropped his eyes to the belt and could see no weapon. Looking beyond the man, he saw two cowhands sitting at a table, their eyes fixed on Jason. Both were carrying six-guns slung low.

'No, you've got the wrong person,' he said firmly, 'I am not your son.'

The man looked hard into Jason's eyes and rolled his tongue around in his mouth as if he was chewing something, possibly his next sentence.

'Well, that's a shame, son, because I was — '

Jason's hand dropped to his holster and the loud click as he cocked his revolver cut the sentence short.

'You don't listen too good, do you?' he said, his eye catching the movement at the cowhands' table. He pulled his gun slowly and pressing it into the cattleman's side said very calmly, 'Now, you listen, feller. I've just come in here for a quiet drink, which I am going to finish. Tell your two boys not to do anything silly or you'll get a drain-hole in your barrel. Do I make myself clear?'

The cattleman slowly moved his hands in an accepting gesture. He glanced back to his boys and nodded his head so they put their hands on the table.

'Look, s . . . ' He nearly said it, but managed to stop himself in time. 'I admire a man who knows how to stand his ground. I'm here to hire and you

4

look like just the kind I want.'

'Well, I'm right sorry to have to disappoint you, but I'm not staying here just now. I have things that need seeing to. So let's just ease up and all go back to where we were.' Jason holstered his gun and finished his drink as the cattleman walked back to his table.

Confrontation was the last thing Jason needed; a gunfight would likely land him in jail if not stretched out on the floor. Filmont was a big enough town to take exception to casual gun-fighting. It was not what he had come here for. As he passed their table he said, 'No hard feelings,' and pushed out though the batwings. He threw the saddle-bags over his horse and urged him into a steady trot.

The streets of Filmont Junction were alive with every kind of commerce. A big bustling town focussed on squeezing every dollar it could out of the cattle trade and every ruse to rob the cowhands of their hard-earned cash. Travellers changed trains here at the end of the main line and headed south towards Texas, or went west to follow a dream. The town was full of hopeful young men from city life in the East or escaping from poor prospects down South, all looking for adventure as bounty hunters and pioneer traders. The reality was a little different and many ended up as drifters in the dozens of saloons and eventually the county jail. Drifting had never been part of Jason's life.

He rode out of Filmont without a backward glance and going northwards, the town was soon left behind and roads became tracks into rough country. Ten minutes outside town limits, Jason took a side track leading to a small outcrop, slid off his horse and climbed to the top. He lay flat and waited, ears turned and eyes peeled. The tell-tale sign was not long in coming, a distinctive distant drumming and wisps of dust in the air. Within minutes the cattleman's two rough cowhands passed below the outcrop at a determined pace. Jason slid back, took out his tobacco pouch and rolled a smoke. He lit it and took a long pull. Before he had finished the smoke, he heard them return at a faster gallop, no doubt heading back to town to tell their boss there was no sign of the insolent upstart, their mission unaccomplished. Jason watched them go, smiled to himself, mounted up and regained the trail.

It had been a timely reminder that Cottonwood County was on the edge of the rule of law and the gun was still preferred to a sheriff's badge for enforcement of the pecking order. It was also a reminder to him to guard his sensibilities. There had been no need to react so violently to the cattle rancher, perhaps he had indeed been hiring hands and Jason would be a good hire.

Standing at a fraction over six feet tall with strong handsome features, dark-haired with deep brown eyes and full lips, well-muscled with fine hands and weighing in at around 170 pounds,

Jason was the epitome of a fine bred athletic young man fresh in from the East. But the gun belt and the .44 Colt frontier strapped low on his leg coupled with the occasional sharp focus of his eyes dispelled any notion of a greenhorn. Jason Colebrook was his own man, and nobody's son, except his pa's, God rest his soul.

Jason continued northwards and late that afternoon he rode into Blackstone, a growing two-bit town, reverberating to the sound of sawing and hammering as new buildings took shape on both sides of the main street. A handful of Mexicans, a long ways from the border, stripped to the waist, were whacking in new planks on the boardwalks to extend the town's possibilities, as yet just a hunch in some tycoon's bag of dreams. Hitching outside the one and only saloon, Jason went up to the bar.

'Glass of beer and something hot to eat if you can.'

'Steak and beans?' asked the barkeep, pouring the beer.

'Just fine. Can you recommend a room?'

He nodded over Jason's shoulder. 'Across the road, where you can get your steak and beans. Three dollars gets a room, a hot bath and breakfast as well.'

Moments later Jason checked in across the road. Then, having put his horse into the livery stable for the night and eaten a satisfying prime cut steak, he soaked in the bath and turned in early. From force of habit he'd checked that the bedroom window dropped straight down into the dirt at the back of the hotel. He hung his gun belt on the bedpost and with the Colt under his pillow, he drifted off into a deep sleep. Amazingly he didn't dream for a single second that night.

For years Jason had been unable to stop dreaming about the fateful day he was on the stagecoach to Danville. It had become a recurring nightmare in which fact and fiction became indistinguishable. He had been traumatized into thinking it was somehow all his fault, that he had been responsible for what happened, that he should have done something to stop it. But he was only a child of eight, what could he have done to stop three robbers?

From the age of fourteen he became a regular visitor at the law firm his pa had set up from scratch and built into a thriving business. Astute and intelligent, Jason had made himself useful brewing coffee, running errands, delivering court papers and four years later he began law studies in earnest. He was determined to follow in his pa's footsteps and become a county prosecutor. Then, getting near to the end of his studies and no longer able to keep the nightmares to himself, he asked his ma to tell him the truth about the stagecoach robbery. After dinner one night they sat together in the kitchen, lit only by the flickering flames of a blazing fire as the light faded outside and shadows danced on the ceiling. The setting somehow added an extra dimension of unreality to the awful truth which Jason was hearing for the first time. Fact and fiction could at last be separated. His nightmares might not stop at once but he had at last some tangible detail on which to rationalize his thoughts. His ma wept as he had never seen her weep and putting his arms round her as she shook with huge sobs, he knew there was no chance of following his intended occupation until he had delivered a more direct kind of justice.

He had carried on his law studies in his pa's firm to please his ma and at the same time he began to prepare for the search. He read through old copies of the Danville Courier to see what the press had to say about the stagecoach robbery. He spent time assiduously studying the court records to see what had been reported of the robbery. Useful snippets were gleaned but nothing gave him the break he needed. His legal work was beginning to pay a small wage with a little left over from providing for his ma and himself, so over the course of a couple of years he took intensive lessons in riding and shooting, and studied fieldcraft, camping out with an old Crow Indian who had opened an enterprising business for would-be frontiersmen.

Then, out of the blue, after years of frustrating research, he came across the lead he'd been waiting for. He saw the name, Clem Marlin, on a wanted poster. The name was surprisingly similar to one that had been reported in the Danville court records of the robbery. Jason made some enquiries and when news came through that a posse had captured Marlin and he was now lodged in a Nebraskan jail, Jason told his ma he had to go and see this man. At first she implored him to leave it all alone as no good could now come of what was long since finished. There was no point in raking over something that happened twenty years ago, but all his plans had now become a reality and it was time to test his resolve.

He packed his bag and kissed his ma goodbye. Putting his hand to her face and wiping away the tears from her eyes, he held her tight and promised to take care of himself. She knew what he was doing and knew she couldn't stop him; in her heart despite the fear of losing him, she didn't want to.

★   ★   ★

Now he was asleep in a small town called Blackstone 600 miles away from his ma in a dreamless place with creaking floorboards and faraway voices drifting on the night air.

He woke an hour or two after sun up and breakfasted downstairs on bacon and eggs with a mug of good strong coffee. Ahead, as far as he knew, lay another fifty miles of mostly easy riding across open spaces, wooded valleys, rocky outcrops and winding streams that would bring him at last to the township of South Bend.

A light spring breeze whipped little

eddies of dust in the street as he rode his horse out of the livery corral and turned toward the north. Folk were already beginning to populate the sidewalks as shutters went up on the stores. Pots and pans were being hung up. Sacks of four appeared in front of a half-finished facade grandly displaying a painted sign proclaiming provisions of every kind and heralding the beginnings of competitive trading. Carts and buckboards negotiated their way between each other, coming in for supplies or, business already done, making their way to outlying spreads.

A man in a grey suit and derby hat stepped out in front of Jason. 'Good morning, sir!' he exclaimed, raising his hat. 'Can I interest you in a plot of prime grazing land? Or maybe a town house? We have many fine plots for sale in our peaceful and law-abiding community.'

Jason shook his head. 'I'm headed up to South Bend, thanks all the same.'

'South Bend! Well, we have an office

there too, young man. Yes indeed, sir, a good friend of mine — one Rosco James by name — is the land agent and he will find you a very good place. Why don't you step right here into my office and I'll give you a letter of introduction.'

Jason reined in and looked at the man for a long moment, chewing something over in his mind. The land agent seemed unsure whether the offer was about to be accepted or a gun pulled to send him scurrying back into his office. The latter certainly wasn't in Jason's mind, he was figuring that every scrap of information might prove useful.

'Sir?' the agent repeated, gesturing toward his office with his hat.

Jason dismounted, hitched his horse and stepped up into the office. He sat down in a large comfortable chair next to the desk. At the back of the office sat another man, clean shaven, probably in his late forties, slow moving with a slight limp and wiry. He was busy stacking papers, but the red bandana round his neck and the polished gunbelt looked like imitating a hired hand rather than an office boy. The agent passed Jason a fine china cup of hot coffee.

'Now, sir, let me tell you today is your lucky day. My name is Jim Tracey and this is my assistant Abe Renton, and I am going to give you a note of introduction to my partner Mr James in South Bend. Yes, sir, a note of introduction. Mr James will find you the very best plot of land.'

Jason let the agent ramble on.

Tracey lowered his voice and looking down, shuffled some papers on his desk. 'I trust you have erm . . . erm . . . arranged the necessary erm . . . securities with a bank of your choice.'

'I have sufficient funds if that's what you mean.'

Tracey leant forward ingratiatingly. 'Of course, sir, of course. Now..Mr . . . '

'Colebrook.' Then Jason leant across the desk too, conspiratorially. 'You see,

I made my money in the East, a few robberies, the odd bank or two, not forgetting a very profitable ransom . . . Now I thought I ought to settle down a bit, make myself scarce for a while or two, buy a spread and raise me some beef.'

Jim Tracey wasn't sure whether to laugh out loud or not. He compromised by chuckling intermittently. 'I see you are a man with a sense of humour . . . '

Jason looked him squarely in the eye but didn't say a word and the agent started to fidget uncomfortably. He took a sheet of paper from the drawer and dipped his pen in the ink pot.

'Well, Mr Colebrook, you won't find us unduly inquisitive, no, sir, we keep ourselves to ourselves out here. Every man has a right to his privacy. Isn't that so, Mr Renton?' His assistant nodded in silent agreement. 'And see here,' he said, handing the paper to Jason, 'this will introduce you to Mr James. Mr James is the man you want. Yes, sir, only Mr James. No other land agent will do.

Remember the name.'

Jason folded the letter, stepped out of the office, put it into one of the saddle-bags, unhitched then mounted and turned his horse again to the north. At that moment there was a scream, a door opened and a woman ran out into the street, her blouse ripped across her back. She stumbled and fell, her arms splaying into the dust, followed by a dishevelled ruffian, his suspenders askew, holding his pants up with his free hand.

'Bitch, whore, where's the money?' he screamed at her, falling upon the hapless woman, no more than a girl by the look of her, slapping her about the head. 'The money?' he demanded, pulling a long knife from his belt.

Jason drew his Colt and fired once into the ground beside the wrestling pair. 'Leave her be!'

'You stay out of this,' the man shouted back, briefly looking up, 'or I'll cut your throat, too.'

Jason fixed the man with a steady

gaze, levelled his gun to the man's forehead and pulled back the firing pin. 'Is there something wrong with your ears? They don't listen too good, do they? Perhaps you'll hear better with a hole in your head. Now leave her be.'

The man let go and took a couple steps toward Jason. Another shot into the dirt stopped him in his tracks. 'If you have a grievance against this young lady, you take it to the sheriff. Personally I can't abide men who rough handle women.'

By this time a sizeable crowd had gathered to witness the commotion. The sheriff emerged from his office. He strode across the street.

'Aww, Bill, you got a problem with Betty? Man, you gotta keep these things to yourself. Now let her up and sort it out decent like. There ain't no need for cutting her.'

Jason holstered his gun and watched to see what would happen next. The man put his knife in his belt, spat into the dust in Jason's direction and that was to be the end of it.

Jason slipped off his horse and approached the man. 'That seems like pretty uneven justice to me.' In a flash he pulled his fist back and delivered a heavy blow. Bill's head jerked back and his knees crumpled beneath him as he fell prostrate into the dust.

'Now wait a minute,' the sheriff said to Jason, 'you can't just . . . '

'Can't what? Do your job cos you're too weak to do it yourself? What kind of a town is this?' He mounted his horse, and glared at the sheriff. 'Certainly no decent place, that's for sure.'

He moved his horse lightly into a trot and didn't look back at the crowd of Blackstone citizens who had barely moved for the last five minutes, but he heard them arguing amongst themselves.

2

Jason was in no hurry. Time didn't matter, a satisfactory outcome was all that he cared about. His quarry was no more than a day's ride away. He envisioned the confrontation, a ranch somewhere away from the town, an exchange of words, a reminder of what happened twenty years ago, an admission of guilt, a confession, then justice could be served. The one big difficulty was avoiding any gunplay; the man that he wanted to bring to justice would not be a man on his own, he would have a retinue of hired hands, of skilled gunmen. Jason knew he would be just one man against them all. If South Bend was at all like the two-bit town of Blackstone he had just left, then it was unlikely he'd be able to call on the assistance of any badge-wearing lawmen.

The track dropped down to a bubbling stream shaded by cottonwoods and aspen. The sun was high in the sky and a blue jay was squawking nearby. Jason steered his horse a little ways upstream and dismounted. He untied the cinch and eased off the saddle then let him graze the fresh green grass. Gathering enough fallen wood to make a small fire, he took some water from the stream into his can and set it down on the wood to boil. Sitting close to the fire, he crossed his legs and pondered. Just now, everything was going well.

Finishing his coffee, he kicked out the fire and retreated further into the wood. Nestling down by a moss-covered boulder, he rolled a smoke and blew out the blue tinged mist, watching it disappear into the green canopy.

His horse pricked its ears first. At almost the same moment Jason sat upright, shifting his holster to a better position. He listened intently, there were no voices, no conversation, there was only one horse. He heard the rider drop to the ground near the ashes of his recent fire. Peering through the tangled undergrowth, he wasn't surprised to recognize Abe Renton. Was he following Jason, and if so, why? All Jason had to do was pull his gun and question the agent's so-called assistant, or he could just leave him be and see what he did next.

Pulling his gun out, he pushed gently through the bushes. 'Howdy, Abe! Looking for something?'

Jim Tracey's assistant held his hands out to show he had no intention of going for the gun which he carried high on his waist. 'I was just curious.'

'And just passing by on the off chance? Where are you headed, Abe? Or were you just told to follow me?'

'Follow you? No, no, I'm taking some papers from Mr Tracey to Mr James at South Bend, that's all. The smell of hot ashes was strong where the track crosses the water so I thought to have a look see on the off-chance of a cup of coffee.'

Jason thought the story not unreasonable but couldn't help suspecting that there was more to it. 'What sort of papers?'

'Land registries, a few claims, that sort of thing. They're in the saddle-bag, you can check if you want.'

'Show me,' Jason ordered. 'Get them out real slow.'

Visibly nervous, Abe Renton opened the saddle-bag. 'I ain't pulling no tricks, mister, I saw what you did to Bill Smithers, you have a strong sense of justice, but hereabouts you better be careful, folks don't like incomers pushing them around. That's all I'm sayin'.' He lifted out a bundle of official looking documents and held them towards Jason. Jason waved them aside; instead he lifted the saddle-bag flap and fished about inside pulling out another folded paper and a wad of bank notes. He dropped the bank notes straight back and opened out the paper. It was a letter from Tracey to Rosco James advising him of Jason Colebrook's imminent arrival in South Bend with a few lurid details about the incident in the street and warning James to be careful. It suggested Jason Colebrook may not be what he seemed and made a hesitant reference to Jason's mention of bank robberies and so on. Jason folded the letter and put it back in the saddle-bag.

He holstered his gun. 'That all seems perfectly OK to me, and you best get going if you're to make South Bend before nightfall.'

'And you?'

'Me? You can tell both Mr James and Mr Tracey I'm just fine.'

The agent's assistant mounted and tightened on the reins but hesitated to go. 'Do you mind if I ask you a question, Mr Colebrook?' Jason acquiesced with a nod of the head. 'There's more than $250 in that wad, but you didn't even look, and unless you're planning to put a slug in my back you ain't touched one copper penny of it.'

'Perhaps you didn't listen up too good. I told Tracey those days are over, I need to settle down, not get some posse scouring the landscape for me. Now scram.' He slapped the horse's flank and it jerked into a quick trot, the hoofbeats soon changing to a regular canter. Looking closely at the ground, Jason noticed that Renton's horse had a distinctive groove on one of its shoes. Such close observation was one of the valuable lessons he learnt from the old Crow.

Jason went back to his resting place and reflected. The upshot satisfied him a great deal, in fact he couldn't have done a better job himself. All he had to do was let Renton deliver the letter to James before he called on him himself. Any story he told James would be believed because he would already have seen it in the letter from his friend Tracey.

Given the rest of the day to ride, Renton would reach South Bend by nightfall. Jason decided to proceed at a slower pace, to sleep out overnight and ride into South Bend later the next day. Having eaten biscuit and some cold bacon washed down with coffee, Jason laid out his bedroll and gazed at the stars. He wondered what his ma was doing, no doubt she was fast asleep beneath these same twinkling beads of light. It didn't occur to him to wonder why he was out here in the wilds of Cottonwood County instead of 600 miles away to the east, looking after his ma and progressing his law practice. He knew exactly why he was here and he wasn't going to question it. Thinking wistfully of home, he soon fell fast asleep.

★   ★   ★

Waking early the next morning, Jason encouraged the embers of last night's fire to struggle back to life with a handful of dry twigs. Once it had recovered its strength, he piled on a few larger chunks and put some water to boil. He carefully rolled some tobacco, lit it, inhaled deeply and throwing his head back, blew a stream of smoke into the sky. He crushed some roasted coffee beans and poured on the boiling water. Taking the last piece of hard cheese and the last two biscuits from his food pouch, he breakfasted, albeit frugally, in high spirits. Today he should reach his destination, maybe even his destiny, and hopefully get a sight of his quarry.

Making sure the ashes were thoroughly soaked, Jason kicked them out, scuffed out traces of his stay as best he could, mounted up and rode out. Following the main trail north, he soon came to an intersection with a signpost showing five miles to South Bend. He decided to skirt round to the west and look at the lie of the land. The rough track climbed up the side of a canyon and brought him out high on a small scrub-covered plateau overlooking the surrounding landscape.

Away to the left the land continued to rise in a range of hills with rocky outcrops and deeply cut valleys. In the east the sun was still low in the sky and spreading its early daylight across a fertile valley with a wide winding river, good stands of mature timber, open grassland, and low hills rising in the far distance. The same outlook was to be had to the north. There the hills became mountains, making the situation of South Bend an ideal spot in the intersecting valleys with a small river port for trade downstream toward the Missouri. The only thing missing was a railway and with the Union Pacific railroad that he had just travelled a hundred miles to the south at Filmont, surely it would come soon and South Bend would boom overnight. For Jason the lie of the land both physically and metaphorically was beginning to fall into place.

All the factors which he had just surveyed suggested to Jason that land prices in South Bend would be high and rising. It could be the best place to invest half the money which his pa had left, sitting as it was in his saddle-bag by way of a bank letter of credit. Thinking it best to enter the town in a peaceable fashion and ensuring that he didn't respond precipitously to any potential threat, Jason took off his gun belt and put it away in his supplies bag hanging over the horse's flank. His Winchester repeater was readily accessible in its scabbard to the right hand side of his saddle, and a small derringer was permanently stowed in his left boot.

The track dropped down into the western edge of the town through timber, mostly blackjack oak, some tall ponderosa pines and a lot of low brush and scrub. It came out eventually on to a wide thoroughfare. Jason was nonplussed by the general air of degeneration, not the thriving town he had expected at all. Riding parallel with the main street, he noticed many half-built structures which had come to a halt, overgrown plots pegged with attached claims, old deliveries of lumber with weeds growing up between the stacks. None of this looked like a town with prospects.

Cutting up between a barber and gunsmith, Jason came out on to the main street and his eyes at once alighted on the prettiest girl he had seen in a long while. Just across the street, she was leaning against the rail on the boardwalk in front of an office. Struck motionless by the combination of deep brown eyes and flowing red hair which she was holding back from her face while tying it with a ribbon, Jason was riveted to the spot. Her tight, orange checked blouse and fawn riding britches accentuated her shapely figure and Jason guessed her age to be around twenty.

Maybe the town wasn't so derelict after all!

Just then a man came out of the office, said something to the girl, kissed her on the cheek and stepped off the boardwalk to cross the street. The girl turned around and went into the office, closing the door behind her. It was only then that Jason noticed the sign painted on the window: Rosco James, Attorney at Law, Government Land Agent, Mining Claims Office.

So maybe that was Mr James's daughter, surely not his wife, and here he was with a letter of introduction and a good biography from Mr Tracey already delivered by the hand of the helpful Mr Renton. Jason Colebrook, masquerading as a reformed outlaw, was ready to be introduced.

3

Much as he wanted to go into the office and introduce himself to the agent's daughter, if that's who she was, Jason felt it would be a sign of bad manners barging through the door without any warning or appointment and putting the young woman in an awkward position while her father was out of the office. Instead he rode on down the main street looking left and right at the businesses which had set up in the town. There were the usual offices for agents of various kinds, commercial enterprises and general stores selling everything from land registry to wills and guns to coffee pots. Then a draper's and milliner store occupying a grand double frontage with barely a handful of hats in the window display and not much to be seen inside by way of cloth or dresses on show — a high class hat store selling ladies' finery but going out of business?

Jason hitched his horse in front of one of the saloons advertising rooms at reasonable rates and good home-cooked food. He pushed through the batwings and went up to the bar.

The barkeep greeted him warmly. 'Howdy, what'll it be, whiskey, beer, mescal, sarsaparilla?'

'I'll have a beer right now, thanks, and I'd like a room for a few nights.'

The barkeep, a tall, well-built man of middle age with a furrowed brow and piercing blue eyes, poured a glass of beer from a barrel tap under the counter and smiled friendly-like at Jason, placing the glass carefully in front of him, and at the same time taking a six-gun out of a drawer and resting it slightly menacingly on the bar counter with his finger near the trigger. 'Tell me what you think, it's my own brew.'

Realizing the man wanted an honest opinion, Jason picked up the glass and examined the colour. He nodded in approval then held it up to his nose which he wrinkled slightly at the sharp odour. 'What's it made from?'

The barkeep rolled his tongue round inside his mouth as if he was tasting it himself. 'The finest ingredients, sir, the finest. What d'yer think of it?'

Twisting the glass round in his hand, Jason was suddenly aware that the room had gone quiet. He turned around and saw that almost all the eyes were intently fixed on him. The room waited with baited breath. Even the poker players had paused to watch. Jason took a fair sized slug and rolled it round his tongue then turning his head sideways, spat it out on the floor. 'Disgusting!'

There was a moment of deep silence in which a trigger cock would be deafening. With angry eyes, Jason looked up at the barkeep and at that moment the whole room burst into laughter. The barkeep put on a broad grin.

'Welcome, stranger! We like honest

fellows in these parts.'

Everything quickly returned to normal, the poker game resumed, the pianist started a new tune, talk rose to the level you would expect and Jason was given a glass of whiskey to take away the foul taste of the odious concoction.

'Now I'll be happy to give you some beer without the vinegar,' the barkeep said, still smiling.

It soon became clear in conversation this was a ritual particular to this saloon. With a newcomer's first glass of anything, the barkeep slips in an appropriate dose of his strong vinegar. It gave the town the chance to measure a stranger. Some fellers drank the whole glass and said it was good so as not to offend the host, and those present knew such men were weak and useless. Some simply swallowed their first mouthful and said they didn't like it very much, making excuses that they were used to something different. Others dealt with it in various ways, including aggressive mistakes. Those like Jason were seen to be men who could be trusted with their opinion and not the sort to be pushed around. Everyone in the saloon determined by a stranger's reaction how they should be treated.

Now drinking a glass of the host's very good unadulterated beer, Jason was glad he wasn't wearing his gun belt. Under normal circumstances he might have been tempted to draw on the barkeep and ask him what his game was. It was a good job that hadn't happened as he felt sure other guns would have been drawn against him and he would have been forced to back down.

The host put his gun back in the drawer and held out his hand to Jason. 'Welcome to South Bend and Patty's Place, my name's Cal Herman and this is my bar. What's yours, my friend?'

'Jason Colebrook.'

They shook hands. 'Glad to know you, son.'

'No,' Jason said firmly but friendly,

'anything you like, but not son. Don't call me son.'

'You got it,' his host replied, 'now if you want a room and meals you'll need to go through the arch there to the hotel and ring the bell. My wife Patty will see to you.'

Jason guessed that while Cal might be the front of the business, the name of the saloon suggested that it was his wife who owned the place. He turned to leave the bar and walked past the poker table into the hotel lobby. His eyes alighted on the man who had come out of the office and kissed the pretty girl on the cheek. Mr Rosco James, perhaps? In front of him was a stack of chips, a pair of cards held close in his hand and five more face up on the table. Three other players had chucked in and just one was facing James, smiling conceitedly.

'What's it to be, Rosco?'

James confidently pushed out most of his chips. 'I'll see what you've got, Zeb.'

'Full house, fives over kings.'

Rosco James put his cards face down quietly and pursed his lips into a tight line of accepted defeat. 'OK, boys, that's me done for the moment.' He looked over to Cal. 'Cash me in, Cal, and keep it on the tab.' He got up from the table. Jason watched him leave, then went on through the arch and hit the bell.

He was surprised when a young woman appeared and gave him a warm broad smile. 'How can I help? Looking for a room?'

Jason nodded, temporarily lost for words. He assumed this was Patty but surely less than half the age of Cal Herman, lucky man. 'Yes, I am, ma'am. Or may I call you Patty? A room for a few days, breakfast and dinner, and a hot bath whenever I want one.'

'I've got a nice room overlooking the street at $5 a night with meals, baths and everything.'

'Sounds good to me, ma'am.'

She smiled with her bright blue eyes and teased him by twisting a wisp of blonde hair which hung down over her eyes. She looked him full in the face, 'You can call me Patty if you wish,' she said, 'but I don't think my mother would be awful pleased.'

Jason felt his cheeks flush bright red and he lowered his eyes. 'Gee, I'm right sorry, miss, only your pa said Patty would attend the ringing of the bell and I . . . well, I just went right on there and assumed . . . '

'Assumed my pa had a pretty young wife?'

'No, not at all . . . well, I mean yes, you sure are pretty, miss but . . . '

'So, you'll take the room?'

'Sure I will.'

She turned to the board and took down a key. 'Follow me,' she said and took off up the stairs.

Jason followed a couple of steps behind. She unlocked the door and pushed it open.

'Will this do, Mr Jason Colebrook?' she said, making it plain she'd heard the conversation at the bar. 'You can call me Riley, if you want to use my proper name,' she said coquettishly, putting the key in his hand. Turning with a flounce of her hips, she closed the door behind her.

Jason pulled back the curtains and opened the doors on to the veranda which ran along the front of the hotel. He stepped out and looked up and down the street. It was early afternoon, the sun was high and hot, there was a bit of activity with carts and horses, buckboards and some smarter carriages. A few people strolled on the boardwalks and several men were just sitting along the street in the shade of an awning or doorway waiting to see how the day would pass. The sheriff's office was halfway down the street on the left. Opposite was a branch of the county bank, its windows grilled and barred. A small group of men stood outside its heavy oak doors deep in conversation. Away at the end of the street, Jason could see a wide flat-bottomed boat bobbing on the water, a ferry to take travellers to the north side of the river.

He was just about to go back into his room when a sudden commotion burst out of the saloon downstairs and spilled into the dust. First off, a body came sprawling into the dirt followed by a stocky fellow who strode over to the scrabbling body and placed his boot smartly into the writhing ribs.

'On yer feet, boy, and find yer gun. I'm counting to ten. One, two . . . '

A crowd soon gathered, coming out of the shops and other places, and even the sheriff could be seen standing outside his door, arms akimbo, but his hands nowhere near his gun.

Just then the girl with red hair ran out of James's office across the street and stood in front of the young man struggling to get up, placing herself between the two of them.

'No, Pinkie, you can't do that, I won't let you, Dale is only a boy.' She held her arms out to shield the lad.

'But man enough to call me a cheat!

An' you're too sweet on him.'

'You shouldn't let him play,' the girl retorted.

This was more than Pinkie was going to stand, he pulled his gun and levelled it at the girl. 'That's enough. I'll talk to you later, now leave me to teach this boy a lesson. Get up and draw, Dale.'

Jason's fingers were twitching. Why had he taken his gun belt off? The derringer would barely make a dent at that distance. It was obvious Pinkie was handy with a gun and judging by the pallor on Dale's face, he knew he was already beaten. Jason's sense of justice bristling, this was surely the moment he had to do something to stop Pinkie, but he had no gun to hand. Without thinking, he grabbed the curtain rod from the window, levelled it like a Winchester and called out, 'Put up your gun, Pinkie.'

Everyone looked up in Jason's direction as it stopped them all in their tracks except the sheriff who Jason could see out of the corner of his eye making his way down the street. Pinkie lowered his gun.

Jason said, 'That don't look to me like a fair fight, whatever he called you . . . And nobody who wants to be called a man levels a gun at a girl.'

Pinkie narrowed his eyes to focus and Jason felt him scrutinizing the curtain pole. Surely he was going to realize quite soon that it wasn't a gun. While Jason was speaking Dale had got to his feet and shielded by the redhead, moved cautiously back to the board-walk and disappeared into Rosco James's office.

Then came the words Jason was not wanting to hear. 'Want to shoot me with a wooden stick?' Pinkie laughed, bringing his gun up to a direct aim. A shot rang out and Jason ducked, splinters of wood from the verandah railing showered around him as he leapt back into the room.

Pinkie would soon be up the stairs so Jason decided to meet him halfway. Pulling the derringer from his boot, he pushed open the bedroom door and advanced to the top of the stairs. Nobody showed up, he listened and heard Cal Herman's voice booming across the saloon.

'Put your gun away, Pinkie Yulen, and go sober up before I make you into a pepperpot. That temper of yours will get you shot one day, now git along outta here.'

Pinkie could be heard grumbling, then he stomped off and all went quiet again before normal saloon noise was resumed.

Jason booted his derringer and went down the stairs into the bar. 'Thanks, Cal,' he said, 'much obliged.'

'No sweat, you done a good thing and Pinkie's just a drunken bully when he's had a skinful.'

'That was a brave thing the girl did,' Jason remarked, 'took some guts to do that.'

Cal poured a glass of beer for Jason. 'On the house. You've just done a brave thing, too. Fiery as her red hair, that girl Fern. Rosco James's daughter, practically runs the business for him all by herself, brains and guts. An awesome combination in any woman. Pinkie treats her like he owns her. An' she's kinda sweet on Dale, too, he runs errands for James and that sort of thing. You probably saw James in here earlier, playing poker . . . '

'I saw him lose a lot of chips.'

'Worst player in the world,' Cal said, laughing as he picked up another glass to clean. 'I don't see him win too often, but he keeps a tab and pays up regular. That's all that matters to me.' He leant forward conspiratorially and lowered his voice. 'Sometimes he spills as much as a few hundred dollars, and he keeps on losing. Those four players at the table, three now Pinkie's gone, take him regular for a good whack every time. An' he keeps coming back for more. Some people don't know when to stop.'

Jason took a swig of beer. Maybe there was more to it than that, why would you keep losing to the same people time and time again? Jason suddenly felt a need to look into the affairs of Mr Rosco James and not just because he had a pretty redheaded daughter called Fern.

4

Jason pushed through the batwings, mounted, and rode his horse to the livery stable where he agreed a price for feed and a week's stabling. He took his saddle-bags, untied his provisions bag and bedroll, pulled the Winchester out of its cover and went back on to the street.

Walking back to the hotel deep in thought, a hunch told him that Rosco James fitted into the picture somewhere, but he wasn't yet sure where or how. He decided that he would spend a couple days just swanning around town to see what he could glean while trying to keep out of trouble. One thing he wasn't going to do was walk around without his gunbelt securely round his waist and his holster secured to his leg; he couldn't risk any unarmed confrontations with the likes of Pinkie, and although he didn't plan to use his Colt, it usually made hot tempered dudes think twice before pulling a gun. He pushed in through the batwings.

'Supper's ready, Mr Colebrook.' Riley beckoned him through to the hotel dining room.

'I'll take it in the saloon if that's OK with you.'

'Sit yourself down and I'll bring it in,' she said, a wide smile spreading across her pretty features.

He took a corner table where he could watch everything — the poker players, groups of drinkers, the regular barflies propping up the counter, groups of friends enjoying a smoke and a chat. So much better than sitting alone in the hotel dining room. Snippets of conversation drifted into his ears and gathered in his mind. Riley soon came in with a plate of steaming beef pie, the aroma tickling his taste buds into a frenzy of anticipation. Having eaten only his cheese and biscuit for the last twenty-four hours, it was a delight to tuck into some good chunks of tasty beef. When he had finished Riley came for his plate.

'That's mighty good home cooking,' he said, brushing her hand as she lifted his plate.

'You have to thank my mother for that,' she replied, hesitating a moment with his fingers resting gently on the back of her hand. Their eyes met and coyly she looked down at once. She took his plate away and soon returned with a cup of good strong black coffee and a noticeable flush to her cheeks.

Jason pushed his chair back, put his feet up and rolled a smoke. The four poker players who all but cleaned out Rosco James earlier were sitting a short distance away to his left. One of them he had already met in a way, Pinkie. Three were of a similar age but the one who took the lead in ordering the drinks and had the last word in their short conversations was much older. The foursome had sat together the whole evening, not inviting anyone to join them and nobody seemed interested in talking to them beyond a polite howdy. Then Rosco James came into the saloon with his lovely red-haired daughter, Fern.

They took a table next to the poker players and James signalled to Cal for a couple of drinks. After a short while the older of the foursome went over to James, who took a folded document out of his jacket pocket and slid it across the table.

'When you're ready, Hatch,' was all James said.

Hatch took the paper, folded it in half again without looking at the contents and pushed it into his pocket. He signalled to the other three who obediently got up and followed Hatch into the street. Jason heard them mount up and ride off.

'Was that another one?' Fern asked her father a few moments later.

'It's all perfectly legal,' her father replied, 'so stop worrying, we'll soon have cleared the way and then there'll be an end to it.'

'It doesn't feel right, they're honest folk,' his daughter replied.

'Honesty isn't the issue. They were offered a fair price, they could have sold up and moved off quietly. It was their choice not to, they knew what would happen.'

Just then Fern looked up and caught Jason's eye; she seemed to recognize him but wasn't quite sure, then it fell into place. She smiled at him and getting up from her chair, walked across.

'Pa, this is the man who saved Dale this afternoon when Pinkie was threatening to turn him into a sieve.'

'Well, stranger,' Rosco said with a wide sweep of his hand, 'come and join us, won't you? Take a seat right here and shake my hand. Rosco James, government land agent, attorney at law, at your service.'

Jason offered his hand. 'Jason Colebrook.'

Jason was expecting James to offer

some sign of recognition, some indication that he had read the letter that Renton brought from Tracey and at least to know Jason's name, but strangely nothing at all. James gave nothing away whatsoever.

'A man who can prevent an injustice with nothing but a curtain pole deserves to be rewarded.' James swung round in his chair and called out loudly, 'Cal, this man's expenses are to be put on my tab for this evening . . . '

'Whoa,' said Jason, holding up his hand, 'that's mighty generous but I pay my own way, thanks.'

James was taken aback. 'No need to get on your high horse, young man, I want to honour your bravery.'

'Well, you can,' replied Jason, 'but not like that. I've come to buy some land here and raise me some beef and you can point me in the right direction. That kind of hospitality I will accept.'

Fern gave Jason a disarming smile. 'I'm sure we can find something very suitable for you, Mr Colebrook. Perhaps we could ride out and I'll show you some of the best cattle land South Bend has to offer.'

'That's a deal,' Jason agreed. 'I'll call into the office in a day or two. Right now I guess it's time to turn in, so I bid you good night, Mr James, Fern.' He got up and went through to the hotel, took the stairs two at a time and went into his room.

Rosco James turned to his daughter. 'Very presentable young man, a man with courage and good manners. We don't see too many like him in these parts. But don't you go getting any ideas about him, Fern, I detect a whiff of danger in his presence, and I can see a shine in your eye. That young fellow is not what he seems, and I'm not too sure about the parts that he's hiding.'

'He's not hiding anything, Pa, you're just imagining too much,' Fern reassured her father while quietly feeling a frisson of excitement as her pa's warning sparked a lot more interest in the stranger.

'Listen, my dear, any man who can grab a curtain pole and pretend it was a repeater and get away with it has a very dangerous imagination.'

★   ★   ★

Jason was sitting on the edge of his bed deep in thought. So, had Renton delivered the letter or not? Had James read it or not? If Rosco James had seen the letter he was playing a cool game pretending not to have heard of Jason, and if he hadn't seen the letter, what had become of it and the other things that Renton was carrying? There was one person who would know the answers to some of this, the proprietor Cal Herman, he was sure to know Abe Renton and whether he was in South Bend the other day. Jason decided to ask Cal in the morning.

As Jason was rolling a last smoke of the day before turning in, two miles south of town four riders swerved on to the track leading into the Circle R ranch. They made their way to the stable block, called a lad out to take care of their mounts and crossed to the house. Hatch Beecham pushed open the door.

'Maria! Maria! Beer and some grub for us and be sharp about it.'

'*Sí, señor!*' came the voice from the kitchen.

The four of them sat down at the table and Maria, a dark-haired beauty from south of the border, soon came in with a tray of four beers. She served Hatch first, then the other three and hurried back into the kitchen, returning shortly with a big china tureen and four plates.

'What's in there?'

'Ees good beef stew, Meester Hatch,' Maria replied, lifting the lid off the tureen and wiping her hands on the front of her clean white pinafore, emphasizing the finely rounded shape beneath her bodice. 'Weeth tomato and 'erbs from garden.'

'Smells good anyway,' Hatch declared. 'Serve the boys first.'

Maria dipped the ladle into the stew and a delicious aroma of beef and oregano filled the room. She put the first plate down in front of Zeb Pinero, the tallest of the bunch and at twenty-six, the second in command after Hatch, who was fourteen years his senior. Dark-haired with a long thin face framed with black stubble, Zeb had the appearance of a Mexican, like Maria. As soon as she put his plate down, he picked up his fork and tucked in. The other two, Red Yulen, affectionately known as Pinkie, and Rawl Colley, both twenty-five, both with regular round faces and fair hair, had the manners to wait until Hatch had been served before they too dived in. Rawl Colley was a finely built young man, lithe and athletic with a cheeky grin permanently hovering in the corners of his mouth, a tease which the local girls found almost irresistible on the frequent Friday dance nights. Pinkie was the complete opposite in character with a scowling expression coupled to a short, stocky build and belligerent manner.

'You've got another job, boys,' Hatch announced after he had swallowed a couple mouthfuls of stew. 'Zeb, I want you to ride south tomorrow and take a look at the place. Keep your distance and have a gander at the farmhouse, count the number of hands. Rawl, you and Pinkie do a wide sweep and get a fix on the head of cattle. It don't sound to me like they've got much, should be a quick an' easy job. We'll leave it a couple days after and see how it lies, then swoop in an' tidy up.'

They ate in silence for a while, then Rawl, finishing his last mouthful, looked directly at Hatch. 'Don't it ever bother you, what we do?'

Hatch took a swig of beer. 'Bother me? Not one little bitty bit. An' if it bothers you it's time you saddled up and rode out, just like the day you drifted in.'

Rawl threw up his hands. 'Aww no, don't get me wrong, Hatch, I ain't thinking of pulling out. I just wonder sometimes if we're right just because we got a piece of paper that says we can push people off the land they've worked and don't want to leave. I mean you can understand that, surely . . .'

Pinkie chucked his fork down with a loud clatter. 'If you ask me you do ways too much understandin', Colley. Shoot first, ask questions after.'

'You're both wrong,' said Zeb, getting into the conversation. 'Talkin' ain't never been no use, whether you do it before or after shooting. You git your orders, you do the job, that's all there is to it.'

Hatch listened for a moment to the sudden flow of moral interchange which went nowhere, then brought the discussion to a close. 'Let's go outside and have a smoke, boys.' He pushed his chair away and gave Maria a playful whack on her shapely rump as she came in to clear away the plates.

'Coffee, *señor*?'

'On the veranda.'

5

After a late breakfast of home-cured ham and eggs, fresh baked rolls and good hot coffee, Jason had a smoke on the verandah outside his room. He cast his eyes up and down the main street of South Bend as it came to life. He was troubled by what Cal Herman had said on the subject of Abe Renton and it puzzled him why he hadn't showed up in South Bend. Where could he possibly have gone? Cal definitely knew Abe Renton and he was plumb sure he hadn't been into town. Jason was pondering on that when he was distracted by a sizeable farm wagon loaded down with all manner of household goods and chattels. It was being pulled by a good looking pair of sorrels, more used to being ridden than driven. It slowed to a halt outside Rosco James's office. The man passed the reins to his wife and climbed down carefully. He threw open the office door with unexpected force and went inside. His wife, her wispy grey hair tied tightly in a bun, sat motionless staring ahead.

Hatch Beecham suddenly appeared from nowhere and approached the wagon. Raising his hat to the woman he called out, 'Sure am sorry to see you going, Agnes. Your beef doing so well an' all.'

The woman looked down at him with a hard-lined mouth and sharp eyes. 'Ain't no good fighting when you're our age. Ten years ago, Barney would have took his shotgun to 'em. But we don't want no trouble at our time of life. We'll manage on the pittance James is giving us. Barney's brother's got some land ways up north, a big spread, and needs some help. There's something funny going on here, that's fer sure, an' we're well out of it.'

While Beecham shrugged his shoulders and held out his hands to show there was nothing he could do about it, the door to James's office slammed hard enough to rattle the glass. The woman's husband emerged, stuffing a small package into his shirt pocket. He spat and climbed up to the seat. Folk came out from the shops to watch them go and stood on the boardwalks, strangely silent. The woman handed her husband the reins and without looking to the right or left, they continued up the street towards the ferry. Jason saw them drive the wagon on to the floating platform, then the ferryman untied the craft and eased it out into the river, pointing it slightly upstream to cross in a wide arc to bring it down to the north shore exactly opposite. Soon the cart was heading up the north trail and the two old folk never once looked back.

The woman's words and her look of bitter resignation fixed into Jason's mind as much as Hatch Beecham's very loud greeting. Had Beecham been showing real sympathy or faking innocence? It had sounded phoney. Jason decided it was time to get up and get going and sort out his own affairs before he too was overtaken by events. He took his gear up to the livery and had his horse saddled up. He secured the cinch himself as he never trusted anyone else with that essential bit of safety. He led his horse out and mounted. Just then Cal Herman's daughter rode by and seeing Jason, reined in.

'Good morning,' she called over, turning her horse towards him.

Jason touched his hat. 'Morning, miss.'

'Riley, please,' she said. 'Where are you going, Jason?'

He wasn't used to young ladies making so free with his name, but then back East you would wait until you were properly introduced. Out here in the West manners were different. 'Just taking a ride out to get a look at the lie of the land.'

'Perhaps you'll let me show you around. What exactly do you want to see?'

Although he had his own business to attend to, it would be ill-mannered to refuse Riley's offer, so Jason accepted and they rode off together, eyes following them out of town.

Not wanting to go directly towards the south which was where Jason wanted to look for signs of Renton, he suggested they head off towards the west and he let Riley lead them up a winding path through groves of mature oak dotted with pine. They emerged on an outcrop above the town.

Riley pulled up. 'You won't get a better view of South Bend.'

'Let's pause a while,' Jason said, sliding off his horse.

Jason climbed up to the top of the outcrop affording a good view several miles to the north and south. Riley joined him, holding out her hand for a haul up the last ledge. He took it and felt the warmth, pulling her up towards his chest. She stumbled into him and he suspected it was deliberate. Her mouth was turned up towards his but that may have been by chance. He steadied her quickly and turned to look out across the fertile grazing, watered by the meandering river. Pointing to the road which came in from the south and the substantial ranch house a couple of miles away to the right Jason asked, 'Whose is that spread? Looks a substantial place.'

Riley shaded her eyes. 'The Baron,' she said. 'Well, he isn't really a baron of course, that's what folks hereabouts call him sometimes, mostly behind his back. It's Richer's place. He's just about the biggest land owner in these parts, several thousand head of cattle, I guess. He owns all that land to the east about as far away as you can see.'

'Impressive.'

'You'll get a chance to see him tomorrow night, he's running for mayor and the two candidates will be addressing a meeting in the courthouse.'

'No wonder his name is Richer with a spread like that. And further to the south?'

'No, that's not his, there's lots of smaller spreads going down the south road towards Blackstone and Filmont, though I think the land has turned sour for some reason. People seem to be moving out. But then I expect you noticed people are moving out of South Bend.'

'Not really,' Jason said, not wanting to give anything away to this girl who might repeat his words without thinking about it.

'It's the railroad, you see. We thought it might one day come to South Bend but it seems it's going about fifteen miles to the west to North River which is only half the size of South Bend. Folk are being offered good plots up there for knock down prices, so some are selling up here and buying over there.'

They dropped down the ledges and walked back to their mounts which were contentedly grazing amongst the scrub.

'Was that what Barney and Agnes were doing this morning, that man and his wife with the cart? Moving their house?' Jason asked as innocently as he could.

'Barney and Agnes? Oh them, no, I don't know what that was about, they had a good beef ranch on the south road, I don't know why they went off.'

'Something about helping Barney's brother . . . '

'Maybe.'

'And that man Beecham, what's he got to do with it?'

Riley shrugged. 'I dunno, he's Richer's right hand man, runs the Circle R for him.'

Jason was beginning to get pieces of the South Bend puzzle, but as yet not enough of it was falling into place. 'I'd like to ride on further now if that's OK with you.'

'Sure, but I best be getting back. Pa always worries if I'm out too long.'

'A big girl like you?' Jason said without thinking, then he caught Riley's eye and her cheeks had flushed bright red. He tried to cover her embarrassment. 'No worries, I won't get lost. I'll see you later and thanks for the chat.'

She gave him a smile and touched his arm lightly before turning her mount and digging her heels to break into a trot. Jason watched her ride away, her blonde pony tail bobbing with the rise and fall.

On his way to the livery stable that morning, in possession of Cal's information about Abe Renton, Jason had walked past the hitch rail outside James's office. He had also walked round the back of the office and was fairly sure there was no sign of Renton's horse having been there. He knew where the next search would have to be and Riley had just now pointed the way for him.

Coming to a secluded culvert, he steered his horse through the pine and scrub and headed south. Soon enough he came to the track which led to the Circle R with its tall timber gate posts and fancy fencing. He slipped off his horse and put the reins loosely over a fence rail. He examined the ground for about a hundred feet down the side where any tracks might remain untouched by general traffic. There was nothing that he could find that looked like Renton's horseshoes.

Jason stood for a while by the ranch gate post. Perhaps Renton had been careful to ride in the middle of the road and ensure his tracks were covered. But why would he do that, and why would he come to Circle R rather than James's office? There was only one name which could connect those things — Richer.

When Jason got on the train a few days ago, 600 miles east of Filmont Junction, the only lead he had was the name of a jailed man, Clem Marlin. Jason had travelled first to the jail in Linken where Marlin was being held and got the sheriff's permission to interview the prisoner. Marlin, a wiry, grizzled man a little more than forty years of age with narrow eyes and a mean line to his mouth, was awaiting his fate with equanimity. Weary of being hounded, knowing there was no escape from the sentence of the court and badgered by frequent visits from the prison padre, Marlin had nothing to lose by dictating the necessary confession for Jason. After years of ploughing through court records and old newspapers, Jason had at last gotten the name he needed and a signed statement that would stand up in court.

He stayed on a few days in Linken until the Federal judge came to town to preside over the hanging which Jason witnessed with a mixture of dismay and satisfaction. Armed with the name Marlin had given him, Jason had travelled near enough another 200 miles from Linken to Filmont Junction, the nearest station to the town that Marlin had mentioned. Then he rode another hundred miles north to that very town — South Bend. Now, sure enough, the central piece of the puzzle was right in front of him. This fancy gate would lead him right down to

Nathan Richer's spread.

He could ride straight on down and confront Richer, but there was still too much he didn't know and maybe Marlin had lied after all to protect his one-time associate. Then, with all the other bits of evidence, Jason thought maybe he had stumbled across something bigger going on. Was there a connection between Richer and Rosco James? Maybe with Renton and Tracey, too? Jason couldn't ride away until he'd taken a good look down this track to the Circle R. He was certain Circle R, its owner and hangers-on, were a big part of the jigsaw, just how big he couldn't yet tell. A hunch told him this was the only place Renton might have come to other than James's office in South Bend. Jason stuck his thumbs in the top of his belt and started to walk down the track, scanning left and right.

Head down, trying to identify any distinctive horseshoes, he soon covered a hundred yards without anything to note. Then his eye alighted on something on the very edge of the track where the rider had veered away, perhaps to let others pass by. Squatting down, Jason examined the tell-tale horseshoes which confirmed his hunch: Renton had ridden this track. Just then he heard horses approaching. Too late to run back, he leant casually on the rail fence and waited. He made sure his hands were well away from his gunbelt to show he wasn't intending any play when three riders on good-looking mounts came round the bend.

'You're on private property, mister. Turn around and git back to the road.'

'Howdy,' Jason began, 'I was just . . .'

Zeb Pinero dropped his hand and pulled a six-gun from the holster, 'Don't talk, mister, just walk thataway.' He pointed back to the road with his gun.

Jason had no alternative but to walk, which he did escorted by Pinero, Colley and Yulen coming close behind.

When they got to the gate, Pinero pointed his gun at Jason. 'Put yer hands on yer head an' keep 'em there. Pinkie, take a look at his pieces.'

Pinkie slid off his horse and took Jason's Colt out of the holster. 'A fine Colt .44. That ain't normal for a peaceful man.' He opened the gun, emptied the bullets into the dust and slid it back into the holster. Then he walked over to Jason's horse and pulled the Winchester. He examined it and emptied that too before replacing it. He turned to Pinero. 'A pretty darn good repeater. I'd say he was a man lookin' fer trouble.'

Rawl Colley then chipped in his bit. 'He was in Patty's last night. New into town, ain't you, mister?'

'Uh-huh,' was Jason's reply. 'Do you mind if I put my hands down? I am not looking for trouble out here and I apologize if I was trespassing. I'll be more careful in future.'

'You're dead right you will,' sneered Pinero. 'Now git goin'.'

Jason calmly bent down to pick up the bullets. Pinero pointed his gun and fired a single shot into the dirt a few feet from Jason who didn't look up but continued to gather the six bullets. Another shot threw up a cloud of dust much nearer to Jason, so this time he stood up slowly.

'Throwing lead at an unarmed man tells me exactly what kind of hustlers I'm looking at,' Jason said, staring directly at Zeb Pinero, 'and next time you pull that piece on me I won't be apologizing for anything.'

Standing right behind him Pinkie pulled his gun. Zeb held up his hand to stop him, but not before Pinkie had whacked Jason on the back of the neck. Jason swung round, but Pinkie levelled his gun.

Rawl Colley intervened, 'South Bend ain't no place for you, stranger, it would be better if you headed north and kept goin'.'

'I might just do that,' Jason said, mounting his horse after he had stunned them into a confusion of inactivity by slowly retrieving all the bullets for the Colt and the Winchester and dropping them into his saddle-bag one by one. 'I might just do that, when I'm done with South Bend.'

He turned his horse and rode off at walking pace, confident they wouldn't slug him in the back. Hoods like that take orders and unless they had an order to kill him they wouldn't dare take such a decision themselves. Jason had gambled that fact all along and their actions proved him right. The next question was to know how they were connected to Rosco James and whether Nathan Richer was indeed their boss. A couple of hundred yards out of their sight he reined in, dismounted and reloaded both weapons.

Back at the Circle R gate the three riders sat astride looking at each other.

'That's one helluva cool dude,' said Rawl.

'Cool or not, I don't take to his swagger,' added Pinkie. 'What was he doin' down the track?'

Zeb Pinero reloaded the two empty chambers in his gun. 'I dunno but I don't like it. He knew darn well he was on private property. Anyways, we've got some stakin' out to do, boys, we'll see what the boss has to say tonight. Come on, let's move out.'

Jason waited until the hoofbeats got fainter then rode back towards Circle R to follow the three riders southwards at a safe distance. Whatever they were up to, he was sure they weren't riding for the sake of exercising the horses.

Later that afternoon Jason walked into Cal's saloon. He passed by one of the poker tables where Rosco James was playing again with the three gunmen. They had their backs to him but James saw him come in. After the poker hand which James lost yet again, he came over to Jason.

'Mr Colebrook, can I get you a drink?'

'Now why would you want to do that?'

James looked a little uneasy. He gestured towards the poker table. 'I heard about your meeting today with my friends here and the misunderstanding . . . '

'I've never yet misunderstood cowardly actions, and if they want to explain them I'm ready to listen,' Jason replied, pointedly rubbing his neck.

'They thought — ' James began but Jason cut him short.

'Thinking is not their strong suit, is it?'

Pinkie Yulen heard that and got up from his chair. Jason was ready for a confrontation but Pinkie came over to the table holding out his hand. 'No hard feelings, mister, I guess I was a bit hasty.'

'You guess right, feller,' Jason said, avoiding the offered hand. 'Let's leave it at that.'

James steered Pinkie back to the card table. They sat down. The first round of chips was chucked in and new cards were dealt.

Well, well, thought Jason, that's quite a turnaround, now why would that be? Somebody must have given the order to treat him decent or leave him alone. Either way, he felt a little bit safer for the moment unless it was just a ruse to avoid suspicion before quietly disposing of him in a dark alley.

6

Friday dawned damp and drizzly with the remains of overnight rain just about dying out at sun up. Jason rose early, breakfasted, had a smoke and pondered the day ahead. The most interesting part would be the mayoral addresses in the evening when he would get his first sighting of Nathan Richer. Or it could be an ideal opportunity to poke around Circle R while everyone was at the meeting in the courthouse.

Just after nine o'clock that morning, Jason entered the office of Rosco James, hoping to meet with his daughter. She wasn't there, but her father was shuffling through some papers and was immediately attentive when he saw who had come in.

'Mr Colebrook, glad to see you, sir, glad to see you. Take a seat. How can I help?'

Jason pulled the chair away from the desk a little. 'I'm looking to buy some land, settle down, raise some beef. I was given your name back in Blackstone by a man called Tracey.'

James's eyes narrowed very slightly and he tilted his head into a quizzical expression. 'Tracey? Tracey? I don't think I know anyone of that name.'

A strange reply which Jason brushed aside. Was James suffering memory loss? 'Well, no matter. I see folk are leaving town so there must be some land hereabouts.'

James stroked his chin then jumped up from his chair. 'Coffee, Mr Colebrook?' he asked with too much enthusiasm as he poured a cup for himself from a pot sitting on a stove in the corner of the room.

'I'll pass on that,' Jason said. 'Listen, I've made my money back East and I want to invest it in something for my children.'

James came back to his chair and carefully placed the cup and saucer on his desk. 'You have children?'

'Not yet.' Jason smiled. 'But I'm not planning on being single all my life. And there are some right pretty girls round here. You have a very fine daughter.'

James smiled then shook his head. 'I'm afraid she's got an understanding with a fine man already. Well now, Mr Colebrook, or may I call you Jason?'

'I prefer not, if that's all the same to you,' he said plainly.

'Just trying to be friendly.'

Jason leant across the desk a little closer. 'With respect, Mr James, I didn't come in here this morning looking for friends.'

'No indeed,' James agreed rather limply. He smiled, pursed his lips into a kind of grin and took on a serious face. 'If you'll take my advice, I wouldn't buy here. Let me tell you why.' He lowered his voice as if about to impart a great secret. 'The railway, Mr Colebrook, the railway. Forget beef, buy land.'

There was a dramatic pause as if

James was waiting for the revelation to sink in. Jason, unimpressed by the statement, waited for him to continue. James stretched his arms out full length to the edge of his desk, pushing his chair back slightly. 'The railway is going to North River fifteen miles to the west of here and that's where you ought to buy your land, Mr Colebrook, and I have many plots for sale. Many prime plots. In six months' time you could sell at say, 200 per cent profit. And I could sell you some investment bonds in the railway if you are looking to make a return over the next two to three years.'

The conversation was taking an interesting turn. It confirmed beyond all doubt that James was running a crooked show. Jason wondered how much information he could pump.

He started the ball rolling. 'Plenty of folks seem to be taking your advice and moving out. Who's buying the plots they are leaving, some of them look like substantial residences?'

James sucked in a mouthful of air noisily.

'Good beef farms an' all,' Jason added.

'Once people knew where the railway was going they wanted to buy land at North River. Simple as that.'

'And as a government agent you have plenty to sell them.'

'Enough for the moment,' James said with a shrug of the shoulders. 'The area round North River needs development. Good land, good soil, good timber and plenty of grazing.'

Jason pressed his key question. 'So who's buying up the vacant plots here?'

James looked away quickly and stared out of the window. 'Client confidentiality, Mr Colebrook, I'm sorry I can't divulge that.'

Jason had a pretty good idea who it might be, but no idea why. He got up to leave. 'So you've nothing to show me around here? In that case I'll bid you good day.' He opened the door to leave and just at that moment Fern was about to come into the office. Jason touched his hat.

'Miss James,' he said politely as he stepped aside before heading towards the livery stable.

Fern closed the door behind her. 'What did he want, Pa?'

'He wanted to invest in some land.'

'And I suppose you tried to sell him some in North River.'

Her father got up from his desk and poured himself another cup of coffee. 'He's a young man with money, he needs advice.' He pondered a moment, wondering how much he should tell his daughter about Jason Colebrook's past, the bank robberies and other criminal activities which had been in the letter Hatch had brought up from the Circle R. He decided it would be best to keep the information to himself. 'He's not the kind of man we want in South Bend, Fern. A man like that could cause a lot of trouble.'

'Because he's not afraid to stand up to people? He's exactly the kind of man we need. Someone who'll put a stop to Richer. Can't you see what's happening to South Bend? It'll be a ghost town soon.'

'Only until the railway ... ' he stopped abruptly and deliberately dropped some papers on the floor.

Fern watched him for a moment. 'Until the railway? Until the railway does what?'

James was aware he had blurted out something he didn't want his daughter to know. 'When the railway comes to North River there will be benefits for South Bend as well. Increased trade, new people coming in, price of land will rise ... You'll see.' Satisfied that he had averted a major disaster, James sat down and relaxed. 'Don't you worry, Fern, I'm taking good care of our future.'

'I'm sure you are, Pa, just be careful. Mr Richer is getting to be mighty powerful and you seem to me to be getting too close to him.'

★ ★ ★

A hundred yards down the street, Jason stopped outside the office of the *South Bend Reporter*. Looking through the window he could see they were busy on the next edition. This would be a good time to have a chat. When people are busy they have less time to think before they speak. He pushed open the door and went in.

A small man in middle age with a mop of grey hair, thick spectacles on the end of his nose and a pen in his hand quickly came across to him.

'Mr Colebrook! Welcome, sir, welcome.'

'You know me?'

'Of course, sir. You are famous already in your own small way. The good Samaritan with the curtain pole? There'll be a small piece about that in the next edition. Yes, sir, caused quite a stir. You, sir, are news with a capital N.'

There was a short pause, then pushing his glasses more securely on to his nose he held out his hand. 'I'm Bern Goodfield, proprietor of this small establishment and proud to be the publisher of news about everything in South Bend.'

They shook hands.

'That's good, because that's exactly what I want to talk to you about.'

'Oh?'

'South Bend.'

'A great little town, sir, and destined to become even greater.'

Jason pointed to the office at the back. 'Do you think we might talk in there?'

* * *

Feeling pleased with himself at having gleaned a few more pieces to the jigsaw, Jason left the newspaper office, took his horse from the livery and slowly rode out west. Going into a gentle trot, he knew he was being followed so he quickened just enough to take advantage of a long bend and jig off into cover. He slid silently off his mount and waited. Pulling his gun, he jumped out into the path of his pursuer.

'OK, hold it right there.'

The horse was pulled up in a cloud of dust.

Jason was flabbergasted. 'Dale? What in hell are you doin', boy?'

'Don' get mad at me, Mr Colebrook. I was just told to see where you was goin'.'

'By Mr James, I suppose?'

'Yes, sir.'

'And why does he want to know that?'

'Gee, I've no idea. I swear it.'

'OK, hop off that nag and let's have a little chat.'

Jason led them into the brush and out on to a grassy bank well away from the road. He told Dale to sit down and stood above him for a moment, looking at his boyish, wide-eyed face. He couldn't be more than twenty perhaps, a couple years more at most, a shock of thick black hair fell across his forehead but there was little sign of stubble on his chin. Did Fern really have a soft spot for such an innocent looking hound?

'How long have you been working for James?'

'Since I was knee-high. They took me in when my ma and pa had an accident and brought me up like I was theirs.'

'So you and Fern are like brother and sister?'

'Kinda, but she's fiery like her hair. I wouldn't want to be wrongsides. And she's right pretty. Anyway she's spoken for, got an interest in one of them poker players.'

Jason remembered Cal saying something about Pinkie and Fern. 'Why does Mr James keep playing with them, he loses all the time.'

'I guess he likes poker.'

There was a long pause while Jason waited for Dale to chew over such an unsatisfactory answer, but Dale didn't seem too bright.

'Anyways I heard Fern saying to her pa that he should stop playing as they were taking back all the money.'

'All what money?'

Dale shrugged. 'I dunno.'

Jason took out his tobacco pouch and offered Dale a smoke which he took. They were silent for a moment. 'What do you know about the railway, Dale?'

'The railway? Mr James is making a lot of money on account of the railway, that's all I know. A lot of money. When we sit down to eat at night, he keeps saying that it'll be different when we move to the East. We'll have a fine house in a fine city and live like we should instead of scratching round here at his beck and call.'

'I thought James had a good business here.'

'We used to, but people stay out of our way now. They don't come to Mr James to write a will, or stake a claim, or even to buy land. They go to McCleery at the other end of town. It's all gone wrong somehow, I can't fathom why. No clients, yet he's making a lot of money.'

'Were you in the office when Barney

came in yesterday?'

'Sure.'

'Only he didn't seem too happy to me. Came out, cussing and spittin'.'

'That's no surprise. They sold out, him and Agnes, sold out to Mr James for less than $100, the cattle an' all, nice little spread at the Bar AB. But they'd had enough, said they're goin' north to work for his brother.'

'Why would they leave a good spread?'

Dale shrugged, he had no answer.

Jason stood up. 'Now listen up good, Dale. You ride yourself around for a bit and then go back and tell James that I went to North River, he'll think I was looking at the lie of the land since he wanted to sell me a plot that way. And don't say nothing else about our little chat.'

Jason applied a little psychological pressure by unnecessarily taking his gun from the holster, checking the cylinder to see that it was fully loaded and snapping it shut. The gesture was

not lost on Dale who nodded vigor-
ously as he mounted up.

'If there's anything I can do for
you . . . ' he said but Jason laughed a
little, not unfriendly.

'I'll let you know.'

Dale rode out. Jason waited a while,
led his horse further into the wood,
mounted and skirted back round the
town to travel south. He never had
planned to go to North River, south
was his intended direction where Agnes
and Barney's ranch, the Bar AB,
needed some investigation.

7

The sun climbed into a clear blue sky and the pungent resinous smell of the pines was dispersing on a light breeze. The frequent noisy arguments of blue jays and raucous crow chatter punctuated the forest stillness. The occasional rodent could be heard scuttling into an underground hideaway. Jason's spirits were high, he was at last on the trail of the man he wanted to bring to justice.

Totally confident in his own capabilities, he was beginning to sort out the people he could trust in South Bend and the people to keep his eyes on. And there were two pretty girls who had caught his attention. Life felt good. The only cloud was that his ma would be constantly worrying about him. He should send a wire to let her know he was OK but to maintain his anonymity from prying ears and eyes in South

Bend, he would have to ride the hundred miles south to the telegraph office at Filmont Junction for that. In a couple days' time perhaps. Lost in thought and before he knew it, he was out on the road well to the south of Circle R. Peeling his eyes left and right, he scanned for a sign to Bar AB.

It wasn't long before he came to a track going off to the left with the remnants of a broken sign knocked to the ground. He pulled up and slid off his mount. Poking in the grass a dozen paces away, he found the other piece of the board and turning it over, read the remaining part of the name 'Bar AB'.

'This is it,' he said to his horse, turning him on to the track and proceeding at a cautious pace.

Scrubby trees dotted the track as it fell away from the main road and soon Jason saw the wide vista of grassland stretching out to the east, broken only by small clusters of cottonwood. In the middle distance the river glinted in the sun as it flowed on toward the Missouri watering this verdant land. Remembering the view when he was higher up with Riley the other day, this ranch must at some point adjoin the Circle R spread. Coming soon to the ranch house which looked well-kept, Jason heard hammering and sawing. A figure came into view, walking slowly from the barn. But it wasn't a saw he was holding, a cocked rifle was trained directly on Jason. Instinctively Jason moved his hands away from his side to show he had no intention of gunplay.

'Hold it right there, mister,' commanded the gun-toting stranger who continued to walk towards Jason. 'This here is private land and you're trespassin'. Turn around and git goin'.'

The man waved his gun in the direction of the track in case Jason hadn't understood which way to go. But he knew right enough. Slowly he dismounted and risking the chance of stopping a slug, he lifted his hat and wiped the sweat off his forehead.

Staring straight into the stranger's

black eyes Jason said, 'I was led to believe this spread was up for sale.'

'Well, it ain't.'

'Mr James said I ought to take a look around.'

'Oh he did, did he? That's a hoot cos it ain't his to sell.'

'We both know that. He's only acting for the owner. And we both know who that is, too. Fancy a smoke?' Jason reached into his pocket and slowly pulled out his pouch to roll one for himself.

'Don't mind if I do. Anyways, what's your name, mister?'

'Ben. Ben Coates,' Jason said, lighting up. He handed the pouch to the other man and watched him roll one, then offered him a light. He noticed the man's hands were rough from manual work: dirt underneath his fingernails, a bruise on his thumb.

Still speculatively fishing in the dark, Jason resumed the conversation. 'I guess he'll want to sell eventually and I could be interested.'

The man spat on the ground and pulled a shred of tobacco from his mouth. 'No ways. This is going to be turned into cattle yards.'

'Cattle yards?'

The man looked closely at Jason, scrutinizing for a clue, but wasn't the figgering kind. 'Listen, I ain't told you nothin'. Now git on your hoss, and skidaddle.'

Jason wasn't going to be hurried. He stood up and made to shake the man's hand but he stepped back and nervously waved Jason away with the repeater.

'Well, if he changes his mind, I'll give him top price right now. You'll let him know, won't you? Coates is the name. Ben Coates.' He mounted up and slowly turned his horse.

'Sure, I'll let him know.'

Jason eased his horse into a slow trot. He knew exactly what the message would be and he had a good idea who it would go to. Soon enough somebody would come into South Bend making enquiries after a stranger called Ben Coates. That was a very profitable quarter of an hour and all for the cost of a smoke. The people of South Bend were being taken for suckers. The two questions were: exactly who was organizing the scam and how many were party to the plan?

★ ★ ★

Friday evening and the town was full. Fancy buggies were being driven up and down the main street, dainty carriages were bringing in people all dolled up in their Sunday best. Less prosperous citizens were on horseback or riding buckboards, some even came in farm carts. The Friday dance in the hall at the back of the Two Peaks Saloon across from Patty's Place was a major event each week. But this week was an even bigger occasion as the dance was being preceded in the galleried court house by speeches from the two candidates for the upcoming mayoral election.

'Are you going to the dance tonight?' Riley called out as Jason walked past the reception desk.

He stopped before going up the stairs. 'I hadn't rightly thought about it. I doubt it, I don't know anyone well enough and — '

'I was hoping we might have a dance . . . '

'Us?'

She blushed. 'Not if you don't want to of course. I'm sorry if . . . '

'I'd like that a lot,' he said quickly to cover Riley's embarrassment as she was looking down at the hotel register to avoid eye contact. No girl would have dared be that forward back East, leastways not in Mitchelton, Jason's home town, and it gave him quite a thrill. She looked up and he gave her a smile, their eyes met briefly and then taking the stairs two at a time, Jason was soon in his room, closing the door behind him, heart racing not from the physical exertion but for an entirely different reason.

He stepped out on to the verandah and watched the townsfolk gathering round the court house. He knew Richer was one of the candidates for mayor, but who was the other one? It must be somebody with either guts or conviction or both to stand against such a powerful man as Richer. Then his eye was caught by two figures emerging from the land agent's office, Rosco James and his daughter Fern. Fern, would she be at the dance? Who would she be dancing with? Was she really already spoken for? Could Jason get a dance with her?

★ ★ ★

The court house was packed. Cigar smoke and noisy chatter rose from the seated townsfolk and accumulated under the rafters, coupled with the rowdy behaviour of the young men hanging over the edge of the upper gallery, tossing pennies to see if they

101

could lodge one on a lady's hat. Jason picked his way carefully up the stairs, avoiding people using the treads as a seat. He found a spot where he could eyeball the dais. Sitting to the left and right of the court bench were the two candidates and their immediate supporters, a proposer and a seconder. Recognizing Rosco James and Hatch Beecham, Jason had little difficulty in guessing the man sitting between them was none other than Nathan Richer himself. Jason took a long hard look as the rugged features etched themselves into his brain. The heavy black moustache, the dark eyebrows incongruously highlighting eyes of a piercing blue, the short scar on the left cheek, and the unmistakeably sneering curve of the mouth giving him a self-satisfied, almost arrogant demeanour.

Then Sheriff Geb Nolan stepped up on to the dais, putting his hand on the back of the judge's empty chair to acquire an air of authority. The room fell silent.

'Before we start this election meetin',' the sheriff began, 'I want to remind you that no weapon is to be uncovered in this court house and no lead to be fired in this place. Now that's out of the way, let's get on with the main business. At the last meeting of the ad hoc town council, it was agreed it was high time we elected ourselves a mayor to look after the civil proceedings of this township and especially to make a bid as capital town of Cottonwood County — '

'There ain't no point in that,' a voice called out, 'with the railway going to North River and Filmont Junction the size it is, we ain't going to be no county town here.'

There was a swell of agreement.

Sheriff Nolan held up his hand. 'Well, let's wait an' hear what the candidates got to say about that. As you all know the election is on Wednesday, so be quick an' get a ticket from my office, an' git yer name crossed off the list. The ticket's got the names of the councillors for the next town council under the names of the two candidates for mayor — '

'It was time you stood down as well,' called an anonymous voice.

Geb Nolan tossed his head in a laugh. 'Sheriff ain't up for election just now, so hush yer noise.' Then turning towards Nathan Richer, he called upon him to make his address. Richer stood up, took off his hat, straightened out his waistcoat, and stepped forward to loud applause. He held up both arms and began speaking before the gathering had quieted down.

'South Bend needs a mayor. South Bend needs someone who can turn this town from a diminishing community to the envy of Cottonwood. In short, my friends, South Bend needs me.'

Loud applause accompanied him. As an opening statement Jason was cautiously impressed, but the man's swagger was too assured; he acted as if there was only one possible outcome on Wednesday. He began to strut around the dais, speaking all the while, extolling more of his own virtues than those of South Bend and firing questions direct into the audience but not waiting for an answer. Yes, it was smooth and well rehearsed, but there was no heart in it, no passion for the community. On the subject of the railway he was very hopeful.

'Now, good folk, let's not be despondent about the railway. We know it's North River's gain but I have been talking to the Union Pacific board and there is every chance of bringing a spur to South Bend in the coming years, and I intend to see it happens. If you elect me I shall open a subscription right away with $1,000 . . . '

This was met with lively approval and a few enthusiastic cheers.

'Imagine a cattle yard and all the associated paraphernalia, right here in South Bend . . . the price of property will go sky high and you'll all be sitting on your own little gold mine . . . '

As he went on bribing the towns-people with hot air, Jason thought about the work that was going on at the former Bar AB and what he had been told. If Richer was already building a yard he knew more than he was saying. Jason longed to shout out a challenge but dared not draw attention to himself. Biting his lip was a test of his patience. His belief that Richer was up to something much bigger than being elected mayor of a dwindling town was confirmed. As Richer finished speaking the applause was deafening, accompanied by whoops and hollas and hats tossed into the air. Was that because they believed his rhetoric or because they lived in fear of Nathan Richer?

Jason was so absorbed with Richer that he hadn't even noticed who was sitting on the other three seats. Looking now to Richer's rival for the votes he saw the bespectacled Bern Goodfield of the *South Bend Reporter* sitting on one side, someone he didn't yet know on the other side and between them decked out so that Jason had to look twice to recognize him was mayoral candidate Cal Herman, joint owner of Patty's Place. This was a big surprise to Jason.

Cal stood up. The applause was encouraging but not as loud for him as for Richer. However, he didn't wave his arms about, nor rush into a flamboyant statement, he waited until the towns-people settled. He stood there for a moment with great presence, his head nodding slowly, and he held the audience with his gaze until they were not just quiet but silent.

He began slowly with careful emphasis, 'Promises don't cost a heap of poop.'

He paused.

'And I'll tell you who here has the biggest heap of poop in the whole of Cottonwood County . . . the man with the biggest herd of cattle you never did see. An' who here benefits from his 5,000 head of cattle? Do you, sir? Or you? Ma'am, do you think you get anything from it? No, we don't. I'll tell you who does. Just you take a look at those two men sittin' right beside him. Our government land agent Mr Rosco James for one. An' he seems to be movin' everybody out of South Bend and encouragin' them to move to North River with cheap land deals. Now, don't that strike you as mighty odd, an' him proposing Richer to be our mayor, the man with the biggest heap of poop this side of the Missouri. And take a good look at the other man. Friendly Hatch Beecham. Many of you don't know Hatch that well 'cept by sight, that's cos you only meet Hatch when you get moved off your land . . . '

'That's a lie . . . '

Cal raised his voice slightly. 'Well, I agree there ain't nobody to prove it, cos they've all been moved off . . . '

There was a ripple of nervous laughter. Richer was smiling but looking distinctly uncomfortable and James mopped the sweat off his brow. Cal hadn't finished.

'You folks aren't blind. You saw Barney and Agnes run off their land only yesterday. They didn't get half a dime in $10 for what their ranch was worth. They didn't leave South Bend for no job up north with Barney's brother. If you ask me, this election ain't about a town mayor, it's about a heap of poop and whether you think you'll be able to breathe when you vote for it to land on you.'

His supporters broke into a loud cheer at that, and Cal didn't stop there, he told them plain what he thought about the railroad. He guessed Richer had bought a swathe of land in North River and was selling it off cheap but at a vast profit. And why sell off land there if the railway was about to go to North River? At that point Richer couldn't contain himself any longer, he jumped up from his seat.

'Nolan, make him sit down, he's had long enough making accusations. This is supposed to be an election meeting, not a list of nonsense accusations. Cal Herman, what has gotten into you? This is supposed to be a fair fight, and you're trying to rake up all sorts of dirty deals.'

'Well, I just got to thinkin' about things an' I figured 5,000 head of cattle, well that's one helluva . . . '

People started calling out things and the temperature began to rise. Once someone questioned Nathan Richer, there seemed to be a strong undercurrent of consensus, but few dared confront him openly.

Sheriff Nolan got to his feet. 'I think that's enough, Cal. We get the gist of what you're sayin' but there ain't no sense in stirring up feelings.' He turned to the audience, gesturing for folk to sit down. 'Let's all stay calm and hear what else there is to say.'

People took their seats and things calmed down while each side's proposer and seconder was given a short time to speak in support of their candidate. Jason listened with interest but his mind was figuring the list of people he might be able to trust. It was time for a long chat with Cal Herman.

But as the meeting came to a close and people began to head towards the dance hall at the Two Peaks Saloon, Jason's eyes suddenly caught the fiery red locks of James's daughter and a smile passed across his lips. Whatever else he had to do better be done before the vote on Wednesday — but right now it sure wasn't no election poking on Jason's mind.

8

The excitement of heated passions from the meeting spilled into the street as the lads and girls made their way into the Two Peaks Saloon along with many of the townsfolk. Husbands and wives arm in arm, courting couples walking close to each other, youngsters already dancing in and out of the adults. Jugs of beer made their way hanging from the fingers of flouncing waitresses expertly negotiating through the throng in the dance hall. The music drifted out through the saloon doors and pulled the people into the hall, their feet already tapping in time. The heated arguments of the meeting were already forgotten by almost everyone with the exception of the two candidates and their immediate supporters. The mud that had been thrown in the meeting had found its mark and some of it would stick. Right now folk were intent only on having a good time.

Jason's eyes were following the bobbing red hair as people passed through the bar and into the large hall at the back. He was keen to find out who was courting Fern, who was it that she was already spoken for? He had an uneasy feeling it was going to be someone he already knew, maybe the hot-headed Pinkie.

The dance hall was a little-known environment for Jason. Back home in the East he had only attended the very tame Sunday school parties as a young lad. He had been aware of his emotions being stirred by the girls' pretty dresses, the colourful ribbons and the fascination of the tightly curled ringlets in their hair. As he grew up, the more formal dances where young men could meet young ladies with parents and grandparents always in attendance was not to his liking. Sure he liked girls good enough. From a distance anyways. He knew they were fun to be near and that their fashionable pinched-in waists gave them an exciting shape. To be fair he hadn't really been in the close company of all that many and his law studies had left little time for socializing.

But then he had always felt himself to be the object of some pity with what happened in the robbery and the things people said afterwards. As an impressionable boy of eight and excited to be accompanying his pa for the first time ever to an important trial, he was traumatized by the event. He could never quite recall what took place and wasn't even certain if he was really there. So he was never quite sure when people came to visit or took time to talk if it was out of pity or morbid interest or genuine friendship. It had made him distrusting, made him keep his distance from folk and made him vulnerable to kindness.

If it hadn't been for his mother's family they would have found themselves suddenly destitute. His pa's wealth, such as it was, other than cash in the bank of which Jason now had half, was tied up in the law business and invested in long term stock and railway bonds which might never pay out. It was only years later that he learnt about the generosity of his Uncle Mort, one of his mother's brothers. It was Uncle Mort who ensured they didn't have to move, Mort who paid for Jason's education and Mort who eventually persuaded his ma that Jason was told exactly what had happened during the stagecoach robbery. It was a horror story he had carried locked away for nearly twenty years, a mental scar, along with the physical scar from that same piece of fatally shared hot lead. In these last couple of years once his ma had told him the full story and unlocked the memory, he had verified almost all the information from searching old newspapers, ploughing through court records and every printed source he could find about the robbery. But there were always some bits of detail missing. And now he knew pretty much the whole story since his recent visit to Marlin in Linken Jail.

The loud clapping and cheering at the end of the first dance brought Jason back to the here and now. He manoeuvred his way through to the bar, waited patiently to be served with a warm beer then took up a position away from the bright lights against the far wall where he could scan the gathering. His eyes soon alighted on Fern's glowing red hair as she was led into the next dance by Zeb Pinero. That was a surprise, he wouldn't have had Pinero down as the man chosen by James for his daughter, or was she doing the choosing for herself? Either way it didn't seem right, Pinero with his mean pinched face, a man who preferred action to conversation, something wasn't quite right there. But Jason didn't get the chance to do any more figuring, a boot tapped his leg and he swung round to be greeted by a proffered glass of beer on the end of an outstretched arm which led back to the smiling face of Bern Goodfield, proprietor of the *South Bend Reporter*.

'Well, what did you make of the meeting?' Bern asked, raising his voice a little above the music and whooping.

'I'd like to know what kinda deal Mr Richer has goin' on with the Union Pacific that he thinks he can get them to build a spur to South Bend,' Jason mused.

Bern just smiled at him then rolled his mouth into the kind of shape that suggests he knows something more. 'After you came to see me I did some more digging into our friend's past and his acquaintances. Guess what? You were plumb right. Nathan Richer isn't who he says he is at all. No, sir, not at all.'

'And Rosco James?' Jason enquired. 'What's the connection there?'

But before Bern could answer a scuffle broke out on the dance floor and everyone moved back suddenly, like water being thrown on a fire and with just as much hissing and cracking. Left in the middle of the room were three figures, Zeb Pinero with his arm tight round Fern's waist and facing up to Red Yulen whose face matched the colour of his name.

'Step away, Zeb, an' git your dirty fingers off my girl.'

That answered one of the questions in Jason's mind.

'We was just having one dance, Pinkie, there ain't no harm in that,' Pinero protested while tightening his grip round Fern and pulling her even closer into his body. 'She was just gittin' a bit lonesome 'til you showed up to dance with her, an' she asked me to take care of her . . . '

'You lying . . . ' were the last coupla words Pinkie was heard to utter before twisting Zeb's hand off Fern's waist and almost pulling it out of its socket. Fern stepped well back while Zeb and Pinkie squared up to each other and started their own circling dance at arm's length.

'Boys! Boys! Enough!' Sheriff Geb Nolan boomed across the hall. 'Folk are here for a good time, go an' settle your differences outside 'n' don't spoil the fun.'

Nathan Richer, who was just behind the sheriff, pushed forward into the space. He stood there arms akimbo, an imposing figure. 'Git out, both of you, gorn out.'

They dropped their fists and realized how silly they looked. Shame-faced, they made their way towards the exit. Pinkie scowled at Fern over his shoulder. The band struck up again and the chatter died down as people regained their partners and began to whizz around the floor in a tangle of arms and feet. Jason stored the new information — there was always a lever or two between people, especially between gang members where a woman was involved.

And thinking of women, where was Fern? Jason slipped through the dancers and in a moment was by her side.

He took her elbow and steered her through the twirling couples before she could object. Putting his arm lightly round her waist, he danced her into the circling flow and gave her a broad smile.

'I hoped you'd give me a dance,' he said.

'You're taking a risk,' she replied, flashing her eyes at him. 'When Pinkie gets fired up he's got a temper more dangerous than a rattlesnake, and like as not he'll be more inclined to take it out on you now rather than Zeb.'

'He can try,' Jason replied with indifference, hoping the protection which he believed he had was still intact.

'Fighting talk,' she replied, 'but then you are a bit of a hothead! And I shouldn't want to be on the receiving end of a curtain pole in your hands!'

They both laughed at the joke. Jason was aware that he was being watched by people who would report the laughter straight back to Pinkie to make trouble. But he didn't let her go at the end of the dance, keeping hold of her and fixing her attention with his deep brown eyes.

'I'm right sorry you're spoken for, Fern.'

She looked down, there was a pause, then as she was about to say something the band began again and they moved into the next dance. She kept looking up at Jason but never said a word while he was scanning her pretty face for a clue. At the end of the music, Dale came up to claim a promised dance with Fern and Jason reluctantly let her go, desperately wanting to say more than he had managed but the words stuck in his throat and Dale spun her away before anything more passed between them.

Bern Goodfield sidled up to Jason. 'She's a right flighty one. Her passion matches the colour of her hair, leastways that's what I've heard.'

'Well, Bern, you just keep digging through your files because I'm convinced there is more to find out about her father. There's something goin' on here that doesn't add up. Why is a land agent selling land fifteen miles away in North River when there's good grazing here? An' why are folk packing up and moving out all of a sudden? I think I know who's buying the land even though James wouldn't tell me.'

'Well, I'll tell you who to talk to, you talk to the man I'm backing for mayor.'

'Cal Herman over at Patty's Place?'

'The very one. Standing right over there talking to his daughter.'

Jason ran his hand through his hair. 'Yeah, I'll do just that.'

At that very moment Riley, by the strangest of coincidences, turned away from her father and met Jason's eyes fair and square.

'And have you registered to vote yet?' Bern quizzed. 'We need all the support we can get for Cal. If Richer becomes mayor because people are afraid to vote against him, this town won't be worth living in unless people are prepared to lick his boots and follow his orders.'

'What? Yes, well.' Jason was distracted, he turned back to Bern. 'Well, I might just be able to do something about that.'

Bern's eyes lit up. 'You think so?'

'I'll tell you what I think — ' Jason began but he was cut short by a tug on his sleeve.

'Shall we?' she asked. Riley's head was slightly cocked to one side and her lips were just parted in a wide smile. Her eyes sparkled.

Jason disappeared into a haze of momentary confusion. 'Shall we?' he queried lamely.

'Dance,' said Riley, laughing at his discomfort.

Bern gave him a little shove in the back which he didn't really need and in a moment Jason had taken Riley into his charge as they moved into position for the next dance.

Three dances later Jason was in a perpetual whirl. He needed a breath of fresh air and thanking Riley for the pleasure of her company, he left the dance hall for a smoke.

Stepping outside, the night air was refreshingly cool. The stars blinked and an owl was hooting. Jason took out his tobacco pouch and moved away from the saloon doors to light up. He was just about to put the flame to his smoke when something metallic was hard pressed into his ribs. He didn't need to turn round.

'Pinkie?'

'Red, to you, mister, only my friends call me Pinkie.'

Jason put the match to his tobacco and drew a deep breath. 'Now let me guess what this is about.'

'You know darn well . . . '

'Until a girl is married I think she can choose who she dances with, don't you?' Jason said coolly.

The gun barrel was pushed more firmly into his ribs. 'That's what you think, mister. Well, let me tell you, you are in a whole lot of trouble here, an' dancing with my girl is the least bit of it.'

'Oh?'

'I'm telling you to ride out of town and don't look back. An' if yer not gone by sun up, you'll be staying here for the rest of your life in an unmarked grave.'

Jason chuckled at the foolishness of the statement as the gun was dug further into his ribs.

'You'll push your luck just a bit too far one day, Pinkie, and until you're given orders to dispose of me you can't pull that trigger even if you want to, so put the gun away and disappear into the night and I might just be inclined to forget all about this little chat.'

'You're darn right you will,' Pinkie said through gritted teeth as he brought the gun down sharply on the back of Jason's head, knocking him clean out and dropping him to the ground like an unstrung puppet.

9

Waking early, Jason quietly got out of bed and pulled on his clothes. Not wanting to disturb anyone in the hotel, he went on to the verandah and climbed over the wooden railings dropping down to the sidewalk. It jarred the lump on the back of his head and he winced. Slipping round the back of the hotel, he made his way to the livery stable and was pleased to see his horse ready saddled and waiting as pre-arranged. He checked the cinch, slipped the groom a dollar and mounted up.

The sun had barely been up an hour before Jason joined it in the already warm morning air. The long shadows stretched right across the road and up the walls of the opposite buildings. He took his horse quietly round the back of the main street and headed out south towards the Circle R. When he last met up with Richer's gang of sidekicks while checking out the Circle R for Renton's hoof prints, they were on their way to a stakeout. There was no doubt it was connected to the eviction which he'd overheard James and his daughter discussing in the saloon. So now it was his turn to do the watching and see if he was right.

He settled on a secluded spot looking down on the Circle R so he could see any signs of movement. As yet all was quiet. It was still early so he gathered enough loose wood to light a small fire and boil some water in the little billycan which doubled as coffee mug. He sat cross-legged and watched the ranch. When he heard the water boil he used a couple of sticks to lift the can off the fire and chucked in some ground beans. The delicious aroma wafted on the air. He stood up, stretched and felt good.

He had only just finished kicking out the fire when there were signs of activity at the Circle R bunkhouse. He couldn't see precisely the faces but there were four men preparing to ride out and more than likely he knew who they were. Then it seemed that only three were mounting up and Jason guessed the fourth was Beecham giving the last minute orders to Pinero, Yulen and Colley. They circled round for a moment seemingly in no hurry to get going. It was soon clear what they were waiting for. Striding across from the ranch house came the imposing figure of Richer himself. The mounted riders gathered together, Richer and Beecham passed a few words then Richer spoke to the three riders. Within a couple of minutes, they trotted out of the yard and on to the track. For a short distance the lie of the land hid them from Jason's view. He climbed into the saddle and waited for them to reappear. As expected, when they passed under the Circle R gateway and got to the main track, they turned south. Jason guessed why everything was focussed on that southerly direction. He just needed to follow them, keeping his distance and his cover.

After some twenty minutes, the three riders left the main track and took to the scrub. Jason took a wide sweep behind them and soon enough came within sight of a small cattle yard and timber buildings. Hobbling his horse, he cautiously crept into a position where he could see the ranch house. He crouched under the low branches of a dogwood and waited.

'Hands up, mister, and don't do nothin' else!'

Jason lifted his hands clear of his gunbelt and raised them high. His eyes were scanning for the direction of his assailant, but he couldn't yet see anyone. Then out of the shadows to his left he saw a young man with a levelled repeater crawl out of cover.

'You're trespassing,' the youth said.

'Easy now, lad, I don't mean you no harm. Is this your land?'

'What's it to you?'

'Is anyone in the ranch house?' Jason asked.

'Why?'

'A whole bunch of trouble is on its way and I don't want to see anybody getting hurt.'

'What do you mean, mister?'

'Have you had an eviction notice?'

'What do you know about that?'

'It's why I'm here . . . '

But there was no need to explain any further. At that moment three horsemen rode into the ranch yard, quickly dismounted and ran into the house. Jason saw the lad's eyes dilate in alarm and flick down to the yard. It gave Jason a sudden opportunity. Moving swiftly, he grabbed the repeater with one hand and swung the boy round so fast he fell to the ground where Jason quickly secured him and held him down. A dog barked inside the house. Two gunshots were fired. The young man struggled to free himself.

'That's my ma and pa,' he spluttered, unable to contain his rage.

'Now hold on,' Jason commanded, 'there ain't no point getting yourself killed. They were just gun shots, it doesn't mean anyone's been shot. An' listen, I'm on your side, understand? So just hold steady. I'm going to ease off my grip, don't do anything silly.'

Jason loosened his grip while still holding the young man, his dark eyes blazing. They both looked down on to the ranch but nothing could be seen.

'What's your name, boy?'

'Matt. Matt Easton and that's our ranch, that's my pa's ranch. Built up from nothin' to what it is, an' we ain't givin' it up without a fight.'

'Was that why you were lurking around up here with your rifle?'

Matt raised his head and looked Jason in the eye. 'You were the one lurkin', mister. Why isn't the dog barking any more? An' who are you anyways?'

'Jason Colebrook.'

'Colebrook? Ain't you the one who threatened to shoot Pinkie with a curtain pole? Yeah, I heard about that.

Maybe you ain't so bad but I don't know if I can trust you.'

'I'm here to help you if you'll let me . . . '

Just then the ranch house door was flung open, the cowboys came out and Matt's ma and pa, their hands tied behind their backs, were being pushed out and manoeuvred towards the barn. Matt's pa must have taken a blow to the head as a trickle of blood was running down his cheek.

'Sonofabitch . . . '

'Just wait, we can't do anything yet. The one that's mounted'll be keeping a sharp eye out. More an' likely looking for you if they know you're about somewhere.'

'I won't let them hang them,' Matt said through clenched teeth. 'If I have to run down there an' shoot 'em all, I will.'

'And end up dead yourself. What good would that do?'

'I can't just stand by and let it happen.'

'Sometimes in life that's all you can do, Matt. Just wait with me here and we'll fix them all right, just wait and watch.' Jason eased his grip entirely and let Matt free. 'The right moment will come, but it isn't here yet.'

'Why don't we just shoot them from here, there's two of us and only three of them.'

'And your ma and pa will be the first ones they shoot.'

They crouched quietly, eyes trained on the yard. Jason was ready to grab Matt if he should make a stupid run for it. The mounted cowboy rode off round the back of the ranch house. One of the gunmen (it looked to Jason like Pinkie) stood outside the barn looking left and right and was clearly a bit twitchy, while the other, possibly Pinero, pushed the two old folk into the barn.

'Well, it isn't hanging,' Jason said. 'One man can't do that on his own without a struggle, so they have something else in mind.'

Moments later, Pinero led six horses

out of the barn and hitched them by their head collars to a post. A rumbling sound from behind the house announced a hundred or so head of cattle as they were steered into the yard by Colley. It was an easy job for one man on a horse as it was all railed from the paddock into the yard. Jason figured this was to be a simple rustling to encourage the Eastons to vacate their land.

'Have you seen any of these three men before?'

Matt shook his head. 'I don't think so. Maybe in South Bend, perhaps. I'm not sure.'

'But they haven't been to the ranch?'

'No, that was an older man, the one who kept delivering threats and then the eviction papers. Pa said his name was Beecham, the Circle R boss.'

'Why do they want you off your land?'

'They made us an offer an' Pa turned it down. Next time Beecham came round with another offer, Pa put a hole through his hat and said not to come again. But he did and the last time he came he brought an eviction notice, but it's our land so how can they do that? An' that's all our cattle.'

It looked as if the three cowboys were about to drive the cattle off the ranch. The Eastons' six horses had been tied in a line. Pinkie took up a position in the front and Colley at the back. They moved the herd forward towards the track. Then Pinero slipped back into the barn while the other two waited.

Seeming like an age, though no more than three minutes passed, Pinero came out carrying a flaming torch. He crossed to the ranch house and went inside. Soon the unmistakeable sound of crackling wood drifted across the divide and then the smoke began to seep out of the windows. Matt made an attempt to break free, but Jason was too quick, grabbing him round the waist and pulling him down. Pinero came out of the house, quickly mounted up and the three of them drove the cattle up the track with the six horses strung out behind. Matt and Jason watched while they cleared the yard and headed up toward the road.

It was then they were both caught by surprise as fire broke through the roof of the barn. This time Jason was too slow to catch Matt and he ran headlong down to the yard with Jason hot on his heels. The sound of the cattle covered any noise and by the time they got into the yard, the cattle and the riders were out of sight, round the bend in the track.

Matt ran straight into the barn. 'Ma, Pa, where are you?'

'Here, son!'

Jason arrived shortly afterwards and the heat was so intense he flung his arm up to protect his face. The smoke made it difficult to see what was going on.

'Jason, over here!'

He followed the direction of the call and came across Matt struggling to release his parents who had been tied to a post. There was a lot of coughing.

Jason took out his knife and cut through the ropes, lifting Matt's pa on to his shoulder and running for the door. Matt was soon behind him, carrying his ma like a child in his arms. They just about made it clear of the crackling inferno as fiery beams began crashing to the floor throwing showers of sparks and flaming splinters in all directions.

Jason and Matt carefully deposited their human cargoes and flopped down on the furthest side of the yard. The heat was intense as the house and barn began to fall in on themselves. Thick black smoke billowed into the air and sparks sprayed all over the yard. Matt's ma was sobbing uncontrollably, holding her head in her hands. His pa, still dazed from the blow to his head, sat without a word, a blank expression on his face, staring at his life's work crumbling to ash, resigned to his fate like so many early settlers had suffered in the time of the Indian wars. It was no good being emotional, life didn't come to an end with every setback or there wouldn't be any ranches in the West, nor any towns, or railroads and growing cities. You just pick yourself up and get on with it.

The one thing that was running through Jason's mind, but he didn't want to say it out loud, was that this was no simple eviction, this wasn't just about a land grab. If he and Matt hadn't been on hand this would have been murder. It put a whole new perspective on the issue and Jason now realized that he wasn't dealing with some small outfit trying to increase their land holding. He knew Richer was a big shot and trying to be bigger still, but he hadn't reckoned on murder being part of his ruthlessness. Unless of course Beecham had taken exception to having a hole in his hat and had given his own instructions.

Jason got up and chewed his tongue in thought.

'Look,' he said, 'you can't stay here. When they've driven the cattle to pasture and secured them they'll be back to make sure they've done their job properly.'

Matt surveyed the sorry scene of burning house, barn and outbuildings. 'There ain't nothin' left that ain't already gone up in flames . . . '

The thickening smoke began to drift around the courtyard. Jason urged the Eastons away towards the wooded slope and on to higher ground.

'There's one thing they haven't finished,' Jason said, fixing his eyes on Matt. 'They'll be back to look for you. Is there anywhere you can all go? You'll need to hide up somewhere safely.'

Pa Easton spoke for the first time. 'There's a shack, out on the pasture, down by the river.'

'No, too obvious. Matt, take your folks back up to where we were watching from earlier and I'll sort something out. I need to get back to town fast. Now listen real good. You stay hidden, no matter what you see goin' on down here. Understood? I'll be back as soon as I can. Stay well away from the property. I'll make sure Richer's men don't come back tonight.'

Leaving them to rue their shattered dreams, Jason ran up the slope to find his horse, mounted and as soon as he was out of the hilltop vegetation, put his heels into the horse's flanks and made all haste back to South Bend.

With the skewbald lathering at the mouth and sweat dripping from the cinch, Jason raced headlong into town.

'Fire! Fire!' he shouted. 'The Eastons' ranch! They need help!'

The town stood still for a split second while folk took in what was being said, then as they looked to the sky and saw the clouds of black smoke, word spread almost as quickly as the fire at the ranch. Horses were mounted and empty buckets thrown into carts as the people swung into action. Soon a trail of willing hands was galloping south. Jason knew it was too late to do anything, there would be only charred timbers and devastation when they arrived but it was the best way to ensure the perpetrators didn't go back while the Eastons were in hiding. Better still, townsfolk witnessing the destruction would serve his purpose well.

10

Later in the afternoon a trail of weary folk filtered back into South Bend. With blackened hands and faces they were sombre to the point of gloomy sadness. Tired and downcast, they shook their heads for news of the Eastons and rumour was that they must have died in the fire as no trace could be found. The pastor rang the bell and the citizens made their way to the little church to mourn the Easton family's fate. The pastor uttered a few words of forlorn hope followed by a short prayer to which the citizens added a fervent 'amen' before a quiet file of disheartened people sloped back into town.

Consoling drinks were being poured in the town's two saloons and Jason had a glass of beer at the bar in Patty's Place where he exchanged some quiet words with Cal out of earshot of the huddles of men chewing over the Eastons' fate and other bad events which an increasing number of local folk seemed to be suffering.

Jason whispered to Cal, 'The Eastons aren't dead, they're in hiding and the fire wasn't an accident.'

Cal carried on cleaning glasses and spoke almost without opening his mouth. 'Was Richer involved?'

'I guess so. At least it was his men who put a torch to the place.'

'He's clearing a path to the south.'

Jason agreed. 'That's what I thought. Why?'

'The meeting,' Cal replied, 'the hot subject, remember? The darned railway.'

Jason nodded. 'Well, I've got a buckboard hidden up just out of town and I'm going to get them to a place of safety where they can hole up for a while.'

'Where you takin' them?'

Jason shrugged. 'I guess they might know somewhere.'

'Bring 'em here,' Cal said, 'we'll put them in the attic, safest place I know.'

Just then Rosco James came into the saloon and walked straight up to the bar. He greeted Cal with a cheery hello and clapped Jason on the shoulder.

'Glad I've found you here, Mr Colebrook. I have exactly the property for you to view. A ranch with the very best grazing, halfway between here and North River. The finest spread you'll see this side of the county and ready for immediate sale. And there's a hundred head of cattle included.'

'Well, that's mighty — '

'Not a word, sir, no refusals. It's all arranged, Fern will take you out there tomorrow morning and you can see what you think. Now what do you say?'

On the point of turning down the offer, that one word, that one name, made all the difference. It changed the prospect from a non-starter to a pleasing proposition. Even if he didn't want to buy the spread, a few hours in the company of James's daughter could be both enjoyable and entertaining, besides which he had a bagful of questions which Fern might be able to unravel.

Jason took hold of James's hand which he was holding out expectantly. 'OK,' he said, and the appointment was concluded.

Cal poured Rosco a glass of whiskey and pushed it across to him. Jason had waited long enough to attend to urgent business and he took this opportunity to leave. He put his empty beer glass on the counter and bade them both good evening. He went through to the hotel side and caught sight of Riley hovering behind the desk. She seemed a little flustered and was looking down, shuffling some things about. When she looked up she gave Jason a broad smile and tilted her head.

'It wasn't so bad, was it?'

'Bad?'

'The dancing, you said you don't, but I thought you did it rather well.'

He felt his face start to redden. 'Hell

no, it was fun, it was just that . . . '

'You don't get the chance?'

He nodded. 'Yes, that's it, it was kinda not quite my thing. My feet get all twitchy and forget what they're doing.'

'It wasn't your feet that interested me,' she said, raising her eyebrows. 'I liked the way you held me close so I wouldn't stumble . . . ' She came round from behind the desk and her mouth pouted in an innocently suggestive manner.

'Yes, well, yes, erm . . . ' And now it was him all flustered.

She moved closer so that they were almost touching and looked up into his eyes. 'And you make sure you take good care of yourself tomorrow.'

He looked at her quizzically. 'Tomorrow?'

'With that lovely redhead.'

'Who, Fern?'

Riley nodded. 'I've heard things . . . ' Was Riley jealous? Surely not, there was nothing to be jealous about. She had obviously overheard the conversation he'd just had with Rosco James. 'And don't forget to take your curtain pole!'

Jason saw the joke and smiled. Shaking his head, he put his hands on her shoulders and leant closer.

'Riley! I need you in the kitchen.' It was her mother. Riley pulled away quickly as her ma appeared. 'Oh hello, Jason, I didn't know you were here.'

'I'm not,' he said, 'just passing through on my way out.'

Patty smiled, then said. 'Only what with the fire out at the Eastons' place, lots of folk are coming in here to eat tonight and I need Riley's help with the stew.'

'Well, make sure to save some for me cos I shan't be back until long after dark.' With that Jason disappeared through the door and vanished into the night.

The temperature had dropped and there was a cool breeze rustling the new spring-green leaves on the cottonwoods. Jason picked his way through the scrubby undergrowth then jogged out to the west where he had hidden the buckboard. He jerked lightly on the reins and the horse moved off at a slow walk. The clanking of the chains and the creaking of the boards alarmed Jason; surely it would be enough to wake the dead. But in reality because his nerves were in a heightened state, the kerfuffle was exaggerated well beyond the low muffled rustling that the cart actually made. The moon was unhelpfully bright and a sharp black shadow accompanied his stealthy progress along little-used tracks. In the night chill Jason's thoughts were with the Eastons who were without warm clothing and he hastened as much as he dared, clanking like a ghost train.

Arriving eventually where he thought they were, Jason whistled the agreed signal and waited. Nobody appeared. He whistled again then slipped down off the driving seat, drew his Colt and crouched down a little way from the transport. Then he heard the broken twigs, then more but softly as if someone was creeping up. A shadow loomed.

'Hold it right there,' Jason demanded.

'It's me, Matt Easton,' came the reply.

Jason breathed a sigh of relief, fearing that something had gone wrong. 'You all OK? Where's your ma and pa?'

'We're over here, Mr Colebrook.'

'Come on then, let's get you back to town.'

'To town?' quizzed Pa Easton.

'Patty's Place,' Jason reassured him, 'Cal's attic. Nobody ain't going to look for you there since you're already 'dead' and they'll assume Matt has long since gone.'

It wasn't long before Jason and Matt were helping the two exhausted old folk up the final flight of stairs and into the cosy attic which Patty had prepared with a jug of water, basin and fresh towels, a lighted candle on the dresser and crisp sheets on the beds. It wasn't the first time this little room had served as a place of refuge. Within moments Patty arrived with Riley and three plates of steaming stew.

'Yours is downstairs in the kitchen, Mr Colebrook,' Riley said as she passed close to him.

Patty put the plates on the table. 'If there is anything at all, just let us know. This cord here rings a bell in the kitchen.'

With that they left the Eastons to a very welcome meal and a good night's sleep.

Jason took his seat at the kitchen table and Riley ladled some stew on to his plate. She cut him a hunk of bread then went through to the bar and came back with a glass of beer.

'I guess you deserve that,' she said, giving him a wide-eyed look, 'you're full of good deeds, Mr Colebrook. I'm beginning to wonder if it was to cover up something else. A darker side maybe.'

'No, miss, there ain't no darker side

to me. What you see is what I am.' He scooped some more stew into his mouth and a trickle of gravy ran down his chin. He wiped it away with his napkin. 'Mighty fine grub your ma makes.'

'Good home cooking, Jason, just like I do myself.'

'Did you cook this?'

'Why, do you doubt me?'

'No, no, I was just curious.'

Riley smiled a broad grin of satisfaction; curious was exactly what she wanted Jason to be.

'Well, I need a couple hours' rest right now,' he said, finishing the glass of beer just as Riley leant across to take his plate and with their heads so close, she planted her lips squarely on his for the briefest of moments.

'You rest up real good, Mr Good Guy, an' I'll see you in the morning. Oh and Ma said you can take all your meals right here in the kitchen with us if you like.'

She turned away to the sink and

started to wash the plates. Jason hesitated a moment not sure what to say, so he paused and turned round but Riley was at the sink with her back to him, then hearing her singing to herself under her breath, he quietly left and went up to his room.

Stretching himself out on the bed fully clothed, Jason soon drifted off with a very pleasant recollection of sweet lips on his and descended into a deep and well-earned sleep. Suddenly alarmed at the ringing of a bell, he sprang up off his bed, crouched by the footboard and instinctively pulled his gun. Everything was quiet. But there was a touch of unreality about it, was he awake or dreaming? A cold draught of air from the window confirmed he was awake but then gradually the scene came back to him. He had been walking across a desolate territory in a dreamscape desert. It was a church bell that had been ringing and when he went to investigate he saw Marlin jerking on the end of the bell rope.

Jason gathered his senses and breathed a deep sigh. Now fully awake, it was a jolting reminder why he was in South Bend and what still lay ahead of him. He pulled the curtain aside, the sky was pitch black dotted with points of silver light. The night was silent, the moon lower but still bright. He guessed it was around four o'clock, the loneliest hour before dawn.

Jason crept out of the hotel by the back door and made his way to the hidden buckboard. Leaving the wagon, he mounted the horse and made his way quietly to the south, keeping well away from the main track and now thanking the moon for shedding its bright light on the ground. He wanted to be out at the Easton ranch at first light when the fire-raisers were sure to be back to survey their handiwork. Positioning himself pretty much where he had first observed the previous day's eviction and cattle theft, he settled down to watch. As the sun began to spread its golden fingers across the forlorn scene, three riders came into view. Jason's eyes immediately alighted on Pinkie Yulen. He wanted a word or two with Pinkie.

He watched them poking around and despairing over the plethora of townsfolk's footprints and the general obliteration of any evidence of whether Matt Easton had been back to check on the ranch. They needed to find Matt so the job could be finished. The three had a parley together then Pinero and Colley rode off, leaving Yulen to kick through the ashes. It was Jason's best chance. He slid down the bank and stole quietly round to the back of the burnt-out barn. He saw Pinkie in the barn searching through the ash, trying to find the remains of Ma and Pa Easton just to be sure they were dead and gone.

'They're gone all right,' Jason said, emerging from the shadows and walking towards Pinkie. Yulen's hand dropped automatically to his holster but stopped mid-air as he saw Jason's Colt levelled in his direction.

'It wasn't my idea,' Yulen said pathetically, 'we were just supposed to turn them out, but they wouldn't go. So Zeb started hitting the old feller but he wouldn't give in, so he started on the woman. Hell, man, they gave us some abuse, it was more than Zeb could stand. So he tells us to tie them up and — '

'Yeah, an' I know the rest, I know the whole darn sordid tale. It's all getting outta hand, isn't it? Well, they're gone and now you're looking for Matt. An' you ain't goin' to find him. So you'd better tell Beecham the plot has failed, or better still you tell that to Richer.'

Yulen looked up to Jason. 'Richer? He don't have nothin' to do with this. You've got that all wrong, mister. You're plumb crazed if you think you can get at Richer like this, why, he's got the whole county behind him. From here to Filmont ain't nobody can touch Mr Richer.'

'I thought he was the boss, it being Circle R where you all hang out. Are you telling me Beecham's in charge of these evictions and burnings?'

'I ain't telling you nothin'.'

'Please yourself. Now take your gun belt off real slow, Pinkie.'

'Red.'

'Pinkie's better. After all we're kind of well acquainted now, having met so many times.'

Yulen's fingers itched to pull his gun, but the odds were against him being quick enough. He undid the buckle and let his gunbelt fall.

Jason teased him, 'Besides, 'Red' is a fine colour for hair and we have a mutual friend with hair that colour, don't we?'

Yulen's lips curled into a nasty shape and he looked as if he was about to take a swing at Jason but thought better of it. 'You lay one finger on her again and I'll — '

Jason fired a single shot into the air. 'Enough, Pinkie, save your blather for someone who might take some notice of you. This ain't the last time we'll meet.'

'You bet it ain't.'

'Now git on your horse and skidaddle. Oh and you can collect your gun belt from Fern whenever you like. I'm riding out with her today. I'll see she gets it. While I try to keep my hands off her . . . '

'You'll pay for this,' said Yulen over his shoulder as he dug his spurs into his horse's flanks and disappeared in a cloud of dust and ash.

11

The dust settled and Jason found himself still standing in the ashes of the barn with his gun in his hand and his mind somewhere else. The image of a young lady with flowing red hair galloping through the pine woods flashed in front of his eyes and he was aware he had been standing there too long. It seemed almost wrong to light a fire amidst the scene of charred timbers and ruined lives but he wanted a few moments to chew over the facts, and that was always helped with a cup of fresh hot coffee and a roll of tobacco. Out of respect for the remains of the Eastons' property he moved off the main yard, found a spot up the slope and gathered enough fallen wood to light a small fire.

He took his supply pack out of the saddle-bag and placed the mug of water in the fire which was turning from a smoking pile to a crackling orange blaze. It was inconceivable that Richer wasn't involved in the evictions. It was becoming quite obvious what was going on. All the ranchers to the south were being bought out or evicted to make way for the railway which wasn't going to North River at all, but coming to South Bend. The cattle yards being constructed at the old Bar AB made it perfectly clear that South Bend was going to be the centre of a major cattle empire for Nathan Richer, who was robbing and defrauding the townsfolk with false information. And he expected them to vote for him as mayor!

The water boiled and Jason chucked in the ground beans, lifted the mug off the fire with a couple of sticks and rolled a smoke while the coffee flavoured up. Could that really happen right under the people's noses without them knowing? There must be more people involved in the cover-up and the spread of misinformation. One name came straight to mind and Jason would be seeing that man's daughter in a couple of hours.

He sat back and pulled on his smoke while questions formed in his mind. If Pinkie was right it would be a tough job making any accusations against Richer. Evidence was needed and there didn't seem to be a whole lot of that knocking about. Jason kicked out the fire and walked over to the burnt-out ranch house.

Fire is incredibly destructive. Almost everything either burns or disintegrates. Metals may survive bent and twisted, and china plates do better than objects made of glass which melt or shatter. What had once been a warm family living space filled with laughter, good cheer and the delicious smell of home cooked food, was now a blackened hole with a stove partly fallen through the floorboards, a disintegrated dresser with a pile of broken plates at its base, bits of charred curtain still adhering defiantly to a hanging window frame and the burnt remains of a large kitchen table and various chairs.

It was the pile of broken china which attracted Jason's eye. He picked over the pieces, some still warm, because a glint of metal had caught his attention. Uncovering the partly black, partly shiny tin buried beneath the china shards, Jason prized the lid and stumbled on gold. Not gold in the form of coin or bullion, but gold in the form of paper, crisp, browned and brittle from the heat of the fire. As the words became clear Jason saw at once it was the eviction notice. Fearful that it might disintegrate, he closed the lid and carried it out to his saddle-bag. He smiled to himself a bittersweet smile. There was no doubt whose signature could be read on the paper, but he really wished that man was not so involved.

Checking his pocket watch, Jason set out for South Bend to his rendezvous with Fern who was going to show him the ranch on the way to North River and, he hoped, answer some questions.

★　★　★

On entering South Bend, Jason stopped off at the livery to swap horses. When people say spring is in the air, or the sap is rising, they mean it as a sign of hope, of renewal, of emergence from the cold grip of winter and the promise of warmer days to come. That was exactly how Jason felt when he saw Fern saddling up.

'Good day, Miss James.'

'Good day to you, Mr Colebrook! A fine morning for a ride.'

The town was just coming to life along with the birds and the rising sun. Carts and carriages started the daily round of delivering people and goods to various destinations. Shopkeepers displayed their wares on the sidewalks and townsfolk perambulated the scene, looking for something to do or something to happen. A pile of newspapers emerged from the office of the *South Bend Reporter* and people gathered round for their copies. Riley came running out of the hotel and across the street, carrying a small package.

'Oh Jason, I heard you were riding out North River way, so I packed some lunch for you. Good morning, Fern, I didn't know you were going, too, otherwise I'd have put in extra.'

Fern forced a smile. 'Someone has to show him the way.'

'An' I'm sure you're just the very person for that, Miss James!' said Riley with an innocent wide-eyed grin.

Fern pulled her horse's head a little too sharply away from Riley and spurring on, called back over her shoulder, 'Come on, Jason!'

Jason took the packed lunch and bottle of beer from Riley, rebuking her gently, 'That was a bit pointed, Riley. There isn't any call for animosity between you two.'

Riley slammed her arms into an

irritated fold. 'Between us two? There ain't nothing between me and her, believe me. You men can't never see what's under your noses, that's what causes anim . . . amin . . . that thing whatever you said. She's taking you for a ride, Jason.'

'I guess so,' he replied calmly. 'I need to check out the ranch.'

'Well, you make sure that's all you check out.'

He kissed his finger and leaning down, planted it on Riley's nose, then pressed his heels into his horse and moved off at a casual pace.

'Takin' you for a ride!' Riley shouted after him but Jason didn't look back, he was touched by her concern but he had some questions for Fern and this was the ideal opportunity to get some answers. She hadn't waited and it took him a good three minutes to catch up.

When she heard Jason approaching, Fern slowed her horse. 'That girl has a sharp tongue!'

'She doesn't mean any harm.'

Fern snorted a breath of disagreement and both horses copied her. Jason chuckled to himself and they rode on in silence for a while as he searched for the right words to start a conversation.

At last he said, 'Can I be direct with you, Miss James?'

'Sounds awful formal to me.'

'What do you see in Pinkie?'

'Pinkie?' she said surprised. 'Pinkie is Pinkie, that's all there is to it. He's good fun, maybe a little excitable at times, but a girl needs some excitement in South Bend.'

'He seems a little wild to me. Does he beat you, Fern?'

'I'm not sure I like that kind of directness. Are you jealous of Pinkie, is that what this is about?'

'Hell no, I didn't mean to pry like that. I apologize. It was just that he was so ready to square up to Zeb at the dance that I thought he might have a short fuse, and what with you being promised to him an' all . . . '

'Zeb and Pinkie don't always get on

so well. And I'm not promised to Pinkie, or anyone else, that's just gossip.'

Jason's heart missed a beat when he heard that and he lost his train of thought. 'Let's hold up a while, I'll make us some coffee. Have you ever tasted hot coffee brewed on an open fire?'

'Can't say I have.'

'There ain't nothin' to beat it.'

Fern watched him gather some wood, light the fire and boil the water.

'We'll have to share the mug, I only have one.' He stirred in the crushed beans and waited for it to cool.

'Do you carry that kit with you all the time?'

'You never know when you might need it and there isn't nothing that beats a hot coffee when you need to sit and think. Besides a smoke, of course.' He passed Fern the mug and she took a sip.

She ran the tip of her tongue round her lips. 'Mmm, that's good. So what did you need to sit and think about right now?'

Jason blushed. 'This an' that.'

'And in particular?'

'What do you know about the railway?'

'Railway!' she said, taken aback, expecting him to be on a more intimate level. 'Was that what you've come to South Bend for? To find out about the railway?'

'No, listen, don't get me wrong, Fern, I'm not interested in the railway, it was something entirely different that brought me here but there's something going on . . . '

'And you feel it your duty . . . Are you a lawman, Jason?'

'Hell no, Fern, I'm just a . . . just a . . . ' He trailed off into a silence of confusion.

Fern got up, brushed the twigs and leaves off her britches and mounted up with her head pointing into the wind and her hair billowing in red waves behind her. Jason could do nothing but stare at her fiery beauty for a moment before kicking over the ashes.

He had barely mounted up when Fern said she wanted to know if he was any good as a rider. She jabbed her horse's flanks, disappearing in a swirl of blinding dust and pressed quickly into a gallop. With Jason making ground all the time they raced the best part of a mile before Fern reined in.

Breathing heavily she slid down, undid the cinch, eased off the saddle and left the horse to sweat freely. Jason did the same but breathing more deeply, took Fern by the arms and holding her tight against a tree, gently pressed his mouth on to hers and found no resistance, just sweet compliance.

'Not bad,' she said as they broke out of the embrace. 'I mean the riding.'

He ignored the remark. 'I've been wanting to do that the moment I first set eyes on you outside the office. When your pa came out and kissed you I thought you might be his wife.'

'Well, you're a mighty patient man,

Jason Colebrook.'

'Yes,' he said and for a moment the image of Nathan Richer flashed across his mind. 'Yes, I am. Some things are worth waiting for.'

'The ranch is about a mile further on and I suggest we go and take a look at it if you're thinking of becoming a cattle baron round here.'

Jason laughed. 'That's the last thing I'll ever be,' he said before checking himself, 'leastways, not for a long whiles yet.' He hoped that was enough of a correction. They jogged on side by side.

'But you know, Fern, this railway thing is bothering me. I don't know why the good folk of South Bend can't see what's going on right under their noses.' She made no reply and he continued his musings. 'Perhaps that's the very reason, just like Riley said, people are so busy looking ahead they don't see what's right in front of them.'

'She said that about the railway?'

Jason dissembled. 'Something of the sort.'

Fern pulled her horse up by a substantial pine gateway, the uprights formed from two pine trunks and the crossbeam a well polished plank with large letters neatly carved into the surface and stained red. The fencing either side was in good repair.

'This is the ranch my pa singled out for you, the best one between South Bend and North River.'

'Let's take a look then.'

They rode down the long approach and a fine ranch house came into view.

'At least this one won't get burnt out,' Jason said, admiring the fine carpentry in the outbuildings and the stockade.

Fern cocked her head at him quizzically. 'Burnt out?' But Jason simply said he wanted to take a look inside. He took a quick look upstairs at the spacious bedrooms and came back down to see Fern silhouetted by the window. For a moment he thought he had glimpsed the future and the idea pleased him.

'Might as well eat our lunch in here,' he said, 'then we'll ride round the land. I'm liking what I'm seeing.'

Fern sat at the table and Jason brought in the packed lunch. Fern declined to share it with him but watched him closely while he ate the food Riley had carefully put together. Jason was chewing on his next questions more than the tasty meat pie. By a stroke of good fortune it was Fern who spoke first.

'What's it like back East? I mean, do the ladies all wear fine clothes and have fancy carriages? Are all the houses built of brick and the bakers make fine white bread and the shops have everything you could ever think of?' The questions flowed on rather like a child's and Jason was perplexed at her innocence. 'Pa wants us to move East when he's got enough money to buy a fine house an' all, but I don't know . . . ' She got up and walked over to the window. 'We're not getting as much business as we used to, people are going to McCleery instead of us and land isn't selling like it used to. I don't know what's going wrong.'

Jason went up behind her and put his arms round her waist. She leant back on to his chest then turned towards his face and they didn't hurry over the kiss. Jason withdrew slowly and looked into her eyes.

'You could came back East with me.'

She sighed deeply. 'It's not that easy, is it? I wish my pa wasn't so involved with Mr Richer. Everything seems to have gone wrong since he got friendly with that man. And when Richer is mayor and lord of everything, is he going to bother about us, me and my pa?'

'Richer isn't going to be mayor.'

Fern broke free and spun round. 'Oh? And what do you know about that?'

Jason shrugged. 'Listen Fern, there ain't no way I can protect you from what's coming, but you aren't going to like what I have to say. Your pa is on the wrong side of the law.'

'So you are a lawman!' she snarled. 'You lying sidewinder . . . '

Jason threw his hands up in the air. 'No, Fern, listen, I'm no lawman, leastways not the kind you're thinking. Yes, I've studied law, I'm qualified to be a lawyer, but that ain't the point. I want to help you. You've gotta understand your pa is in this real deep.'

Suddenly all her fears became reality and recognizing the truth of what Jason was saying, Fern hugged herself, crumpled into sobs and fell back against the wall. Jason helped her to a chair and sat her down.

'I'm not the only one who knows what's going on, Fern. The railway isn't going to North River, it never was, it's coming to South Bend just as soon as Richer has cleared the path. That's why folk are being evicted or burnt out. Why do you think Agnes and Barney moved out? The Easton fire was no accident. Why is your pa enticing people away with cheap land in North River and lies about the railway? You know Richer is building a mighty big cattle yard at what was Circle AB . . . '

Fern held up her hand to stop him. 'And you think my pa is involved in all this burning and killing? He wouldn't do that. Maybe he isn't too smart, but he isn't that dumb, either.'

'It's not a case of being dumb, I just don't think he realizes what's happening, or he is turning a blind eye to it. Or maybe he just thinks it is the way to get that big brick house out East and make you a fine lady. Don't you ever ask yourself why he's playing poker every night and losing to those rats? That's how they get paid, his way of paying them. It looks legitimate, a game of cards, but it sure ain't what it seems. And where is the money coming from, Fern? Richer of course. I've got evidence, Fern. I found eviction papers at the Easton ranch. Your pa's name and signature is on them — Rosco James, Attorney at Law.'

'No,' Fern said, slightly dazed, 'that's

not true.' Her brow furrowed quizzically then hardened into an angry glare. 'You're trying to trick me into saying something. I don't trust you, Jason Colebrook, not one bit.' She got up, pushing the chair away wildly as the tears began to blur her speech. 'You just keep your false accusations to yourself and stay right away from me and my pa. Get yourself back East before it's too late!' She ran to the door and slammed it behind her. Jason went to the window and saw her mounting up. He bit his lip because he knew he must let her go.

He cleared up the remains of the packed lunch which Riley had so thoughtfully put together for him and pondered on her words about what people don't see. Perhaps he had done just that and shown Fern what she knew was there but didn't want to acknowledge. Either way she was pretty cross — cross and pretty in fact — and his heart burnt a little for her pain. Had he said too much? Would she go blurting things out and ruin everything before all the evidence could be put together and Richer charged with fraud, deception, intimidation and everything else, even murder maybe? But then he laughed a wry laugh under his breath. There's no need for all that, that's a sideline, the currants in the cookie. He didn't come to South Bend about a railway. He came to South Bend about a stagecoach.

12

There was no hope of catching up with Fern so before making his way back to town, Jason decided to take a tour around the pasture belonging to the ranch. Maybe he could see himself as a cattle baron after all. He sat up straight in the saddle and imagined a spread with hundreds of fine Aberdeen cattle, maybe thousands. And in the ranch house, a family that looked up to him, a wife and children, yes, even a little girl with red hair maybe, just like her ma.

With the image fresh in his mind he rode up to a rocky hillock for a better view down the valley. The pastures were green from the winter rain, the stands of cottonwood were beginning to take on their summer foliage, the aspens were already sparkling and there were good stands of pine on the ridges. The sun was glinting on a large lake away in the distance still part of the spread. Jason smiled to himself. Yes, indeed, this could be the life for him when everything was resolved.

His expression changed suddenly as he spied a distant enclosure. He remembered James saying there were a hundred head of cattle included in the sale, and he didn't need to go any closer to know exactly where they had come from in the last few days. Then he saw a horse tied to the railings and knew there must be someone down there. He steered his horse silently into the woods and descended towards the field.

Close enough to walk the last hundred yards, he dismounted and left the reins hanging. The horse began munching on fresh spring grass as Jason crept quietly through the undergrowth. He squinted at the stranger's horse; he'd seen that saddle before, so where was the rider? That was when he saw the second horse tied almost out of sight and two figures standing nearby engaged in close conversation.

Recognizing both people, tension dissipated, then he hesitated a moment, undecided whether to interrupt them. He couldn't quite hear what they were saying and carelessly moved a little closer, snapping a twig underfoot. Zeb Pinero immediately swung round and pulled his gun.

'Put 'em up,' he barked.

Jason held his arms well away from his gunbelt and stepped forward. 'Easy, Zeb.' But Jason's eyes were on the young lady standing alongside as she glared at him.

'Jason?' she said, her brow furrowing at the intrusion.

'I saw the horse and came down to see what's going on.'

'Big mistake,' said Zeb, moving closer and lifting Jason's Colt.

'Zeb, there's no call . . . ' Fern began. 'You don't need to . . . '

'I'm not going to, he's your fancy friend with a prying inclination. You can.'

'Can what?'

Zeb waved his gun towards his horse. 'Go and fetch the rope off my saddle and tie his hands real good.'

Fern had no alternative but to comply with the order. She avoided Jason's eyes as she walked past. She tied his hands behind him and while Fern and Zeb rode, Jason was forced at gunpoint to walk back towards the ranch. Riley's words about being careful and not trusting Fern were ringing in his ears, but there was little he could do about that now.

Taken back into the ranch house then down the stairs into a cool basement, Jason was told to sit against the wall. Zeb gave his gun to Fern to keep Jason covered while he secured his legs and arms.

Zeb stepped back, dusting off his hands. 'I guess that'll keep you out of the way for the next few days while we decide what to do with you. Poking about in other people's affairs don't usually do no good.'

'We're not going to leave him here like this, are we?' Fern said.

Zeb looked up at her, taking back his gun. 'You got a better idea?' But Fern made no reply. Zeb kicked the sole of Jason's boot. 'Mr Beecham wanted to ask you a few questions, so just wait here until we've finished our poker game tonight and I'll be back with him and the boys to see you're OK.' Pinero laughed too loudly. 'You better have some real good answers ready.' He pushed Fern up the stairs and closed the door, cutting out almost all the light.

Hearing the horses ride away, Jason began to wriggle and twist but nothing gave. Even if he could get to his feet, hopping up narrow stairs was likely to end in a fall and broken bones, or a compound fracture and bleeding to death. There were no windows in the basement, it had been constructed as a place of last retreat in the event of a highly unlikely attack by Indians or some other hostile group. Four small

181

horizontal slits were sited in the very top of the walls, probably affording a limited view in all four directions and just wide enough to accommodate the barrel of a Winchester, but Jason had little hope of standing upright, let alone peering out. And what use would that be in any case? The ranch, empty and deserted, was too far off the North River track.

A smoke and cup of hot coffee would be more than welcome right now!

The light outside was gradually fading as the sun dipped somewhere behind North River. The temperature in the basement was dropping and his limbs were beginning to get stiff. His mind kept running over various escape scenarios, but none of them felt the least bit likely. Keeping himself to himself as he did in South Bend, there was no reason why anyone would even notice he wasn't there. He wasn't looking forward to an interrogation by Beecham. Perhaps Pinero was bluffing, but it seemed unlikely. He even thought he might welcome the beating, just to offer some hopeless and unlikely means of escape. Any action would be better than being trussed up like a roasting hog.

When he wasn't thinking about how he was going to get out of this predicament, his mind kept returning to Fern. Sure she didn't have any choice but to do what Zeb told her, but why was she down there talking to him in the first place? She must have known Zeb was there, maybe had even arranged to meet him. And she must also know about the cattle, surely she must know that. Come to think of it, what was it Bern Goodfield had said to him at the dance — 'She's a right flighty one, her passion matches the colour of her hair.'

Yes, but that didn't prove she was a double-crosser. If she were to tell Pinkie that he was lying here so he could come and give him another buffaloing, that would be a different matter. Or there again if she could see her way clear to come back and cut him loose that would prove despite everything she really did care about him. On the other hand, after all the things he said about her pa, she'd realize he was a danger to her as much as to Zeb, Pinkie, Colley and Beecham. What would she make of all the conflicting evidence? His mind kept going round in circles.

There was only one way to fathom all this; his legal training had taught him to review the evidence carefully and without jumping to conclusions, to be dispassionate and analytical. But the thought of the billowing red hair and the soft compliant lips kept distracting him and eventually he slumped into a doze.

It was pitch black when he woke and he had no idea where he was, not until he tried to move and found that he was severely restricted, then it all came flooding back. He was cold, unbelievably cold. He shook his muscles, tensed them and relaxed, tensed and relaxed again to get the blood moving. A modicum of warmth spread through his aching limbs. Suddenly all his nerves were on edge as he strained his ears into the darkness and there was an unmistakeable softness of step from the hoofs of a horse being led quietly and very slowly by a closely held head collar. So Fern hadn't abandoned him after all. He heard the door of the ranch house being opened, but no footsteps entered and the door was closed. Why would she do that? She knew he was in the basement. Perhaps she wasn't alone. The blood rushing round in his ears confused all the sounds. It couldn't be Beecham and the gang, they wouldn't bother about being quiet.

If not Fern then who? Or perhaps Fern going cautiously in case Beecham and the gang had already come back.

If only he could stand up. Should he risk calling for help? It was becoming obvious the person or persons didn't know he was in the basement. Was it someone looking for him, or maybe a casual ridge rider looking for somewhere to hole up. Either way, this was his best chance, he came to a decision and called out.

'Anyone there?' he shouted, not wanting to call for help as that would give a potential enemy the advantage. There was no reply. 'Who's there?'

Silence, then a click at the top of the stairs as the door was slowly opened and lantern light flooded down into the basement.

'Jason! Jason, are you OK?'

'Sure,' he said. 'Never felt better. Leastways now you're here. Am I glad to see you! How did you know?'

'And I'm glad to see you, too,' Riley replied, leaning down and kissing him full on the lips while he was tied up and couldn't resist. 'I had a good juicy piece of best beef waiting for you in the kitchen, but you never showed up. I waited and waited and then guessed something might be wrong. I knew you had come out this way to see a ranch with Fern so I've been riding round for an hour or so trying to find it. There were no lights here, so . . . here I am. And here you are.' She leant down and kissed him again.

'I find myself at a slight disadvantage, miss. Now if you'd be kind enough to cut me loose, I'd kinda like to get my circulation going again.'

Outside in the cold night air after a few explanations, Jason whistled for his horse but nothing happened. He whistled again, still nothing.

'Maybe they took it with them,' Riley suggested.

'No, it was free when I left it, I didn't tie it or hobble it, they wouldn't have caught it.'

Just then they heard the horse snorting as it broke through the cover and came running up the hill into the yard.

'That's the boy!' said Jason, grabbing the horse by the nose and greeting him by blowing up his nostrils. The horse jerked his head and moved his soft mobile lips rapidly as if scolding him for not taking more care of himself. Jason could only imagine what the horse might say.

'I know, I know,' he said, 'very careless of me.' Then he turned to Riley. 'Now listen, I can't come back into town just now. Tell your pa I'm going down to Blackstone to get a warrant and see he lets Bern Goodfield know as well. Beecham and the other three who play poker every night with Rosco James will be on their way out here later to ask me a few questions — and rough me up — so mind you don't run into them on your way back.'

He mounted his horse and turned up the track towards the road, then stopped, dismounted and walked back to Riley. 'And thanks, you saved me a beating. Take care, those men are dangerous, keep out of their way.' He scooped her up and gave her a quick kiss.

'It's the women you need to take more care over,' she said to his back and he wagged a finger in the air to acknowledge the advice.

13

Jason rode off into the darkness. Riley mounted up and made her way back to the North River road and turned east towards South Bend. She kept just off the track in case Beecham and his men should appear suddenly. She didn't know that Jason, a little way behind, tracked her to Patty's Place to make sure she got back safely. Dismounting and tethering his skewbald, Jason crept close to the buildings and peered through a window into the saloon where he saw James and the gang still engaged in their poker game. He had plenty of time to leave the area before they discovered he wasn't still tied up at the ranch.

Riding at a leisurely pace, he came within striking distance of Blackstone just as the sun was breaking through the clouds and beginning to touch the hilltops with its rose-gold fingers. The sky turned from black to smokey-grey then deep blue before rays shone through, dispersing the wispy cirrus and heralding a clear spring morning. Time for coffee, a smoke and a plan of action.

The first person he wanted to talk to was an old timer who had tried to bushwhack him on his last visit to Blackstone. Abe Renton would be the most likely to crack first and he had the key to some important information. But before he could get to his feet and kick out the fire, Jason was overcome with the exertions of the night, the pleasant releasing by Riley and the l   f sleep. The latter caught him unawares and temporarily closing his eyes, he quickly sank into oblivion.

Dreaming of the fire at the Easton ranch, Jason was struggling into the barn with smoke enveloping him as he grabbed Pa Easton and stumbled towards the door. But the smoke overcame him and he choked violently, dropping the old man in the process. Waking with a jolt, Jason coughed and spluttered as the vestiges of acrid wood-smoke drifted into his nostrils and he was soon on his feet, kicking out the last of the smouldering cinders. In an instant the dream world disappeared into the reality of a forest on the outskirts of Blackstone with the midday sun casting very short shadows. Irritated at his slumbering but feeling much refreshed, Jason mounted up and began the descent into the town. His plan was to talk to Renton well away from land agent Tracey and pump the man for what he knew. Near enough to walk the rest of the distance, Jason tied up his horse and made his way to the main street.

Exactly as a few days ago when he put up at the hotel, the general turmoil and hubbub of a town under construction was noisily continuing. Hammering, sawing and shouted instructions filled the air as the bare-chested Mexicans raised timber frames and put finishing touches to the high false fronts of the growing town. There was a steady flow of wagons laden with sawn lumber, some also loaded with prefabricated sections from catalogues. But one building in particular attracted Jason's attention. It was set a short distance off the main street on the northern edge of the town. A long low building with a wide raised walkway. There was only one kind of building it could be and Jason headed towards it.

'Thirsty work,' he said to one of the Mexicans who was sweating profusely with drops running down the side of his face.

The Mexican nodded but didn't say anything, looking down and getting on with the work as the foreman, a swaggering American dude, strolled over. 'Are you holding up the work, mister?'

Soon Jason was in deep conversation with the man who became more friendly as they chatted. He told Jason that a railroad was about to be constructed just as soon as the last papers were signed and then the spur coming up from Filmont Junction would get underway. There was apparently a short delay due to some late land deals going on further north but as soon as this building was finished he would be moving on with his team of Mexicans to build the next stop.

'And where's that?' Jason asked innocently.

'I can't say, mister. Not until the route is fixed.'

'Well, that's just my point,' said Jason, kicking the dirt with the toe of his boot. 'You see I've got a cattle yard under construction at South Bend and I was hoping you boys would be up that way by now building me a station. I've got a lot of money invested in this enterprise.'

'I know, mister. I've got others saying the same, people on my back all the time about it, and I'll tell you the same as I tell them, nobody is supposed to know about the route, but we'll get there as soon as we can. There's more labour on the way and once those papers are signed, I guess I'll get my orders and then things'll get going a bit quicker.'

Jason chewed over his thoughts for a moment, dare he risk the gamble? The opportunity was in his grasp, should he take it? He must.

'Only I was talking to my partner Nathan . . . '

'Nathan Richer? You're his partner?'

'Yeah, the very same, an' he's getting a bit twitchy. He's coming up for election on Wednesday and he wanted to be able to tell the people that South Bend was definitely getting its railway.'

The foreman threw his hands in the air. 'I know, I know. Mr Beecham was down here only the other day saying the way was now all but clear as the last ranch had sold up.'

Sold up, Jason thought, yeah that's one way of putting it. He held out his hand to the foreman. 'Thanks for the chat. It's put my mind at rest for now.'

He turned to go but the foreman touched his arm,

'The route, as you well know, has been secret for a long time,' he said, 'and hasn't been fully cleared by Mr Richer. Anyhow, give him my good wishes for success in the election, though I don't suppose he needs 'em as I imagine it's virtually a foregone conclusion.'

'Yep, I guess so, all done and dusted.'

Jason left the gang to their work with his mind anything but at rest. It was a gamble and it paid off. That's all that mattered. Everything he suspected had been confirmed and a whole heap more dirt besides. The only problem would be if news got back to Richer or Beecham that someone had been poking around the construction site at Blackstone asking questions and saying he was Richer's partner. His best defence would be to deposit some information with the town sheriff, to cover his back. Even though the sheriff seemed a bit weak last time Jason exchanged words with him after the Bill Smithers incident, he was after all the town's representative of the law and being that way professionally inclined, Jason had great trust in the rule of law.

Merging into the background, Jason made his way stealthily to the rear of Jim Tracey's office. There were two horses tied to a hitching rail. Recognizing one of them, he stroked its nose then running his hand down the horse's flank, he lifted the foot to confirm the mark on the horseshoe. There was no mistake. He crossed to the back window and peered through. He saw Tracey sitting at his desk with a client but there was no sign of Abe Renton. Then he appeared with a cup of coffee for the client, placed it on the desk, exchanged a few words with Tracey and came towards the window. Jason ducked, the back door opened, hiding him from view and Renton stepped out. He closed the door and jumped out of his skin at the sight of Jason.

'Abe!' said Jason, all friendly-like.

'Mr Colebrook . . . '

'Well, you even remember my name. I'm honoured.'

'What can I do for you?' Renton said nervously, fiddling with the packet of tobacco from which he was about to roll a smoke.

Jason looked at the shaking fingers. 'Roll one for me as well and we'll have a little chat while we walk.'

'Walk?'

'You know, Abe, just so as we can sit ourselves down while you tell me what you know.'

'That won't take long,' said Abe, managing a half-chuckle.

'No,' said Jason, 'it won't.'

They walked a short distance towards the edge of the clearing and finding a sizeable log out of sight, they sat and chatted. Leastways, Abe did all the talking for a good five minutes.

'That's all I know, Mr Colebrook, I ain't holding nothin' back from you. I swear it.'

'Well, let's be clear. You delivered the

letter to James just like Tracey said you should?'

'I did.'

'And what exactly did James say?'

'Nothin', I didn't wait for him to open it.'

'I could put a bullet through your lying tongue right now, Abe, and nobody would know. And I don't suppose anyone would care.'

Renton looked up and the colour drained from his cheeks as if it was being washed down by a snap rainstorm. Jason slowly took his Colt from the holster and cocked the firing pin.

'You never delivered to James, you went straight to Richer, or Beecham. So let's start again . . . Why not to James?'

'Listen, I'm just the courier, I don't know nothin' about it.'

Jason grabbed Renton's leg and placed the barrel of the Colt directly on to Renton's boot in the very centre of his foot. 'Yes, you do, why did Tracey tell you not to go to James?'

Renton held up his hands. 'OK, OK,

I'll tell you what I know. They think James is going to back out of things, maybe even give evidence. He wants to get out of the deal and move East. Red Yulen, he's one of Beecham's men and is friendly with James's daughter and well, James knows too much, they think he's a risk. Yulen is going to take his daughter as hostage to keep James quiet if anything happens.'

'Is that it?'

'An' you smell of the law,' Renton said. 'Mr Tracey didn't like your story, you don't look like no bank robber, so I was to go and warn Beecham about you . . . and that's it, Mr Colebrook. I really don't want nothin' more to do with any of it.'

Jason eased the firing pin and slid the Colt back into his holster. 'Thanks for the smoke and the chat, Abe. You're a decent bloke, an' I guess you want a quiet life, so take my advice: gather up everything you've got, saddle up and ride out before it's too late. An' don't breathe one word of our meeting or I'll come looking.'

Jason watched him walk away, unsure he would heed the warning. What did it matter anyway? The thing uppermost in his mind was Fern and the danger she now seemed to be in without knowing it. He sat a while longer, pondering on what information he should deposit with the Blackstone sheriff. He would rather deposit it with Sheriff Nolan at South Bend who would surely execute any warrant on Jason's evidence, but right now he couldn't be seen in South Bend on account of being sought by Beecham and his boys.

Richer had to be stopped before the election took place, if not, he might be too powerful to touch. Maybe he already was on the railroad issue, but not on Jason's other charge. He decided to cool off with a beer while he determined his next move and headed for the batwings of a saloon.

Taking his glass of beer, Jason chose a table in the darkest corner away from the main bar area. Quaffing a long gulp, he didn't notice the nod which the barman gave to one of the customers who slid off his stool and left the saloon. Satisfied with all the evidence he had gathered in this short visit to Blackstone, Jason was metaphorically patting himself on the back for a very successful piece of work when suddenly a figure burst through the batwings and walked across to Jason with a six-gun levelled at his forehead.

'Got you now, you four-flush tinhorn. Get up, mister, and lay your gun real slow on the table.'

Jason spilled his beer as he pushed the table back but the other fellow had the advantage and Jason didn't try to draw. The customers in the bar pulled back out of the way, a couple with their hands ready to pull their guns.

'Now I'm the one with the gun, an' you're left looking silly. How does that feel?'

Jason said nothing but he didn't lift his gun. He recognized his assailant, it was the dude who was beating up the woman when Jason put a stop to him and then laid him out when the sheriff wouldn't take any action. Once again the fellow had had too much to drink and that made the situation doubly dangerous. Jason decided to act cool. He put out his hands away from his gunbelt and opened his fingers to show there was nothing in his hands.

'The gun ... real slow,' Smithers repeated.

'Listen, Bill,' said Jason, 'I'll take the gun out, but when I do, there'll be just one shot an' that will go straight through your brain. It will be self defence and there are plenty of witnesses. What do you want me to do?'

Bill Smithers licked his lips, clearly undecided; should he risk it, this man might after all be a gunman. He was caught in a quandary. Jason was lowering his hands so slowly Bill didn't see the danger. Just then the batwings burst open again.

'Bill!' said a girl's voice and he turned round.

It was just the exact right moment. Jason pulled and there was just one shot, not going through Bill's brain but aimed at his forearm, smacking into the muscle and making him howl with pain. His gun flew across the room. Jason turned on the customers at the bar.

'I said there'd be just one shot, so don't nobody get any smart ideas, there's five more bullets waiting,' he said, waving his gun. 'Girl, go and get the sheriff.'

14

Sitting in the sheriff's office with Bill safely locked in a cell groaning while the doc sewed up the hole in his arm, Jason said he didn't want to press charges. 'Just let the dude sober up and maybe take his gun away for a while.' The sheriff smiled. Jason hadn't got any time for Bill Smithers and his stupidity, there were bigger things at stake and having decided how to proceed, he discussed his evidence with the sheriff so that a warrant could be drawn up.

'You're lucky his girl Betty was prepared to stand witness for you, nobody else would have. It could have been you in the cell instead of Bill. I guess she remembers when you laid Bill out to save her from a beating.'

Jason snorted. 'Bill's the lucky one, Sheriff. Lucky he's still alive, I had every right to put the bullet through his head.'

'Well, that's all over with.' He pushed a paper across the desk. 'Now look here at your statement. You're sure you've got all the right details?' said the sheriff, handing Jason the pen. 'Cos I can't change anything once the warrant is drawn up. So sign right there if it's all true and I'll get a pair of deputies to go to South Bend and serve the warrant. The county judge is due in Filmont in a couple weeks, you'll be around then, I guess.'

'I guess so,' Jason assured him, signing his name on the papers and smiling wryly to himself.

They shook hands and Jason turned to go.

'Next time . . . ' croaked a shaky voice from the cell.

Jason paused. 'Yeah, right. See you again, Bill. Meanwhiles you make sure you take good care of Betty . . . '

★   ★   ★

Feeling a little peckish, Jason decided to get something to eat. Not wishing to tempt fate by relying on his reputation as a dangerous adversary who had just bested Bill Smithers again, he avoided the bar where half a glass of beer was still waiting on the table for him, and chose another saloon across the street. He ordered a hearty meal, not having eaten anything very much since Riley's packed meal the day before. He washed it down with two glasses of beer before mounting up and setting off. Riding behind Main Street, Jason noticed that Renton's horse had gone. He reined in, hitched his mount and went through the back door into Tracey's office.

'Where's Renton?' he demanded as Tracey looked up, startled.

'Why, Mr Colebrook, good to see you, sir! I trust . . . ' he said, pushing his chair away from the desk and standing up. But he didn't get beyond halfway as Jason pressed him back down into the seat.

'Trust indeed!' said Jason, 'I wouldn't

trust you to buy me a newspaper. You're in this up to your neck and you'd better start talking — '

The door to the office opened and a smartly dressed middle aged couple walked in.

'Mr Tracey,' began the man, 'we like the property you're offering. We've had a look round and it's just what we are wanting . . . '

Jason walked across to them and politely taking the lady's elbow, steered them back towards the door and ushered them out.

'I'm sorry but that property has been sold and Mr Tracey is now closed for business today. Call again tomorrow.' He gently shut the door on them and looking at their puzzled faces through the glass, turned the sign from Open to Closed.

Tracey's face reddened with anger. 'You can't just — '

'Oh yes, I can. Now where's Renton?'

'I've no idea.'

Jason slowly took his Colt from the

holster and cocked the firing pin in front of Tracey's nose. 'Talk.'

⋆ ⋆ ⋆

Riding out of Blackstone, Jason felt pleased with the day. He had achieved all that he came to do and more, but where should he go next? To return to South Bend just yet would be highly risky but he needed to get word to Fern that she was in danger. Renton had a good two or three hours' lead on him and he knew he wouldn't be able to stop him getting to Beecham and spilling the beans. He wouldn't forgive himself if Pinkie's plan was put into action and Fern taken as a hostage.

He had no alternative, he had to go to South Bend and hope he wasn't too late.

The sun's rays raked low through the trees casting long shadows. The evening air was cool on his face and the gentle wind fluttered the young green leaves like confetti at a wedding. Jason had no liking for Rosco James but he could see the man had been duped, was nothing bigger than a useful pawn in Richer's game, and now both he and his daughter were in serious danger. Both were dispensable and when chips are down that's the last thing anyone wants to be. He wondered what sort of a beating he would have been given if Riley hadn't found him first. Was he also to be detained, hostage fashion? Or worse still, was he an opponent to be eliminated? One thing was for sure, the stakes were so high this wasn't a game, it had become a matter of survival.

Deep in thought, Jason was careless of the fading light and the distance he was covering so quickly. He realized too late that he should have approached this point more carefully. Just ahead was the small junction where he was going to take the left hand turn and head into the hills to approach South Bend from the forested slopes on the west. From there he could slide down into the town under cover of trees and darkness. This was the point where he would leave the main road, the place where he might have turned left or right, making himself more difficult to track. But it was too late, the rider emerged from the undergrowth with a Winchester squarely aimed.

'Put 'em up!' said Zeb Pinero, keeping the barrel steady on Jason.

Jason held his horse still with his knees as he raised his hands. Pinkie Yulen and Rawl Colley slowly rode out of the shadows behind Pinero, then another figure walked out of cover and approached Jason.

'I rode all the way out to the ranch on the North River road to see you, Mr Colebrook. It was going to be a special occasion but you ran out on me, why was that?'

'I just can't guess,' said Jason. 'Maybe I didn't fancy seeing the ugly side to your good nature.'

'Shall I give him a taste, Mr

Beecham?' asked Pinkie in a whining voice, slipping off his horse with a coiled rope in his hand.

'No,' replied Beecham, 'we'd best save him for Mr Richer.' He turned to Jason. 'He's real keen to meet you.'

'Me, too,' said Jason but he wasn't so sure it was an invitation he wanted.

With Jason securely bound and his horse tied behind Beecham's, the party moved off towards South Bend at a gentle trot and this time there wasn't anyone who could come to his aid. It wasn't comfortable riding ten miles with hands tied together and looped round the pommel. Jason was glad of the lessons he'd had, a lesser rider would likely have slipped off the saddle and had to run alongside with his hands still tied to the pommel. In one way he was glad when they turned into the track down to the Circle R, and in another way he wasn't.

They all dismounted and hitched up outside the bunk house. Beecham freed Jason from the pommel but kept his hands tied. Maria came to the door and stepped out.

'Dinner eez ready now, Mr Beecham.'

'Feed the boys, Maria, I've got some talking to do with Mr Richer and our guest here.'

'Eez he eating, too?' Then she saw the rope around his hands. 'Ah.' She went back in, followed by Pinero, Yulen and Colley.

'This way, Mr Colebrook,' said Beecham, leading him across the yard to the house. Opening the heavy oak front door, he stepped back and signalled Jason to enter.

There was a warm aroma of candle wax and the dry smell of lamp oil. The hallway was brightly lit and the furnishings spoke money. Fine carpets covered the polished wood floor and gilt-framed oil paintings adorned the walls. A bowl of flowers hinted at a woman's touch. Perhaps Richer had married and maybe he even had children. Then a pair of fine mahogany doors opened at the end of the hall and Richer was standing there with hands outstretched.

'Mr Colebrook,' he said in a warm, welcoming and friendly voice, 'we meet at last!' He saw the rope still round Jason's wrist. 'Hatch, the rope. Mr Colebrook can't hold a glass like that. Now come on through and sit down, Jason. I may call you Jason, mayn't I? We've some business to discuss, you and me. Brandy, whiskey, something else? What's your choice?'

Richer led them into a large study with panelled walls and many paintings. The shelves carried a display of European porcelain figures, there were books covered in fine red morocco and an array of small silver objects which glowed in the warm candlelight. But the fine objects were mixed with incongruous displays of old guns, a finely plaited bullwhip, a moth-eaten red and white check bandana and a hat with two large holes in the crown. A strange mixture indicating a man with money, a taste for finery and old world culture, but with an attachment to a wild past that he was reluctant to relinquish.

Nathan Richer opened a small cedarwood box on the desk and offered Jason a cigar which he declined. Richer took one for himself and bidding Jason to take a seat, crossed to an old Chinese lacquered cabinet which he opened to reveal two shelves stacked with bottles and fine cut glass tumblers and wine glasses. Wanting to keep his wits about him, Jason opted for a cold beer but Richer insisted on something stronger and gave him a brandy. He sipped at it, tilting his head while keeping his lips closed and it looked as if he was drinking normally but little passed into his mouth.

Beecham sat in a high back leather armchair near the door, glass in one hand and cigar in the other, perfectly at home, while Richer perched himself casually on the edge of the large, heavily carved desk. He took a long pull on his cigar and blew the smoke in a continuous exhalation.

'We're worried about Fern,' Richer suddenly said quite calmly while looking straight into Jason's eyes. 'Fern James, Rosco's daughter, the one with red hair that you've taken quite a fancy to.'

'Oh,' said Jason, without showing much interest. 'Yes, I know who you mean.'

'She seems to have gone missing and we thought you might know where we can find her.'

'Me?' Jason looked surprised. 'Why should I know where she is?'

'Well, we presume it was Miss James who came back to cut you loose and so you must have been the last person to see her alive.'

Jason leapt up but Beecham was on him before he could get out of the chair.

'You see,' said Richer, 'I knew you'd be just as concerned as we are.'

'Now you listen here, Richer, if

anyone touches a hair on that girl's head . . . '

'Yes,' Richer continued, 'and it's such a pretty shade of red.' He nodded to Beecham who held Jason's hands out in front of him. Richer slid off the desk and tied Jason's hands again. 'Just a sensible precaution, Mr Colebrook. You're a bit of a hothead and we don't want you to get over-excited. I thought I could trust you to behave like a gentleman, but I see I was wrong.'

'It's too late for this, I know all about your plans for the railway and why you've been evicting people or burning them out. You won't get away with it. There's a warrant out for your arrest.'

'Yes, I've heard about that, Jason. That was very foolish. I expect you thought it would stop me being elected mayor.'

'Maybe, but Cal Herman has got more support than you think . . . '

'Cal Herman?' said Richer, unable to hide his surprise. 'Cal Herman is a good friend. He's only standing against me to made it look like a fair fight. No, you've got it all wrong, son . . . '

The word. The one word which would raise Jason's hackles. He leapt out of the chair and took a wild lunge at Richer with his bound hands swinging like an axe, but hopelessly off-balance he landed only a glancing blow and fell to the ground. Beecham pulled a gun on him and he lay in a fit of raging fury.

'I was going to offer you a deal,' Richer continued calmly, 'but I see you're not in a listening frame of mind just now. I want to know why you've taken it upon yourself to interfere in my affairs. What has South Bend got to do with you? Or what have you got to do with South Bend? I intend to find out, Mr Colebrook. I think it would be better to keep you out of the way for a couple days and then you might be ready to listen to reason. You'll find I'm not an ungenerous man . . . Hatch, fetch the boys and see Mr Colebrook safely to one of the guest rooms.'

Just as Jason expected, the guest room turned out to be more like a prison cell in one of the outhouses. The doors were securely locked and bolted and he was hogtied to ensure he stayed put, but at least he was on a mattress and had a blanket against the cold night air. Otherwise there was little to be thankful for.

Dear Lord, if only Riley could perform miracles, now would be the time he had most need of help. It was almost as if he was back to square one, the only difference being the venue. And his worry about the plight of Fern. Was Richer bluffing that she was missing, or had she taken Jason's advice and got out of South Bend before it was too late? Somehow Jason couldn't see Rosco agreeing to that and Fern wouldn't leave without her pa. But then she betrayed Jason soon enough when Pinero demanded her assistance at the ranch, although generously he still thought she had no choice.

We always have a choice, he said to himself, look at me, making the wrong choices is exactly why I am here in this fix. In an unusual flood of self-pity he drifted off into a fitful doze. Then suddenly he was wide awake, ears straining in the darkness. There was a noise. A bolt was pulled back very slowly, a key turned in a lock, muffled footsteps, another bolt, another key, and then the door began to open very slowly, inch by inch.

15

A thin line of candle light cut across the floorboards and drew a hazy yellow vertical on the wall. Spreading slowly, it suddenly filled the void as a dark shape entered the room and quickly closed the door. Jason half opened his eyes. With his heart thumping, he could just make out Rawl Colley standing at the end of the bed. Colley hesitated a moment, looking down at Jason, then put the candle holder on the floor and took out a long knife. Was this how it was all going to end, quietly having his throat cut in the still of the night while all the world slept and nobody would notice his demise? He wasn't going to give up his life without a question.

'Colley?' he whispered. 'What . . .'

'Listen, mister, I don't know what your game is but the others have been discussing how you should be got rid of and it don't feel right to me. There's lots about what we're doing that don't feel right and I don't want to be no part of cold-blooded murder.'

'What about the Eastons?' said Jason. 'You were there.'

'I didn't want Pinero to put them in the barn . . . '

'But you didn't stop him.'

Colley started to cut the rope round Jason's legs. 'Yeah, well, we don't always do what we should. It takes a lot to stand up sometimes when you know others are against you.'

'So what's the game now?' Jason asked.

'I'm getting out. I'm trying to do what's right. I don't want no part in any more murder and that sort of thing. So, perhaps the least I can do is set you free to take your chances. You're against Richer, right?'

'Yes, I am, but not just because of the railroad.'

'Then at least I can let you do

whatever you have to. Are you a lawman?'

'No, but I'm trying to bring Richer to justice. Colley, when you ride, make sure you ride real good, cos Pinkie and Pinero will hunt you down.'

'What about Mr Beecham?'

Jason exhaled a snort of disgust. 'I'll be taking care of him . . . Sshhh!!' Jason indicated the door and signalled that he could hear someone on the stairway. He lay down and Colley put the blanket over him, snuffed the candle and crouched low on the further side of the bed. The door was pushed open and a dark silhouette with a drawn gun stood on the threshold. Not a word was said, but two figures suddenly leapt up and tackled the intruder, bringing him down to the ground with a thud. Jason delivered a punishing blow to the back of the head, the body jerked then lay still.

A moment later a figure was gagged and bound and laid on the bed under the blanket, facing away from the door.

It looked exactly as it was when Colley came creeping in, but it wasn't . . . this time it was Pinero in the bed, not asleep but unconscious.

Colley said, 'You gotta watch that one, mister, he's a mean sonofabitch without any morals.'

Jason pushed Colley towards the door. 'You'd better get going in case Pinkie wonders where he's got to.'

'No, Pinkie'll be fast asleep. He had a real struggle getting the girl out here.'

'Girl?'

'Yeah, James's daughter, Fern with the pretty red hair.'

'She's here?' Jason queried.

'In the basement of the ranch house.'

'And Pinkie, where's he?'

'Asleep in the bunkhouse,' said Colley.

Jason paused for a second. 'One last thing, Colley, tell me exactly the layout to the basement.'

Moments later, they were both outside in the cold night air. Colley was silently leading his horse and Jason was tiptoeing across the yard to the house.

The moon was high and bright, swaying trees cast eerie shadows across the buildings and with each eddy of wind, the fresh young leaves shuddered in the trembling air like riffling a deck of cards. An owl swooped across the yard and hooted with surprise on seeing a human figure. Jason gained the verandah and gently turned the handle on the front door. According to Colley the only locked door would be the one into the basement room and the key would be hanging close by on a hook. Jason slid inside to the hallway, carefully removed his boots and made his way with silent footsteps through two rooms to the basement door. His ears tingled with the sound of his own breathing and the steady beat of his heart. A clock was ticking rhythmically on a shelf, the only external sound Jason could hear. The hook was easy to find by touch but there was no key on it. Jason felt around the doorway for another hook to no avail. Then his heart jumped into his throat.

He crouched down and listened at the door, looking at the keyhole. The key was in the lock on the other side of the door. He was puzzled momentarily, then it dawned on him that there must be someone else in the room. Why would that be? It must be well past midnight. Perhaps one of Richer's men could be in there to keep close guard on their hostage. Or Pinkie! What was he doing in there? Jason pushed the horrible thought out of his mind. He could rush in and overpower Pinkie, and then what? Maybe a crash to wake the whole household and another body trussed up in bed? Everything would be discovered in the morning anyway. It served no purpose. Then again he could finish Pinkie for good, but that would have to be rather unpleasantly done with his knife and in any case he had no hard evidence that Pinkie had committed any serious crime. He didn't want to be judge and jury on innocent, or partly innocent, fools.

What to do?

In any case he might be completely wrong about it all. By God he was wrong! This wasn't the basement door. He had miscalculated the number of rooms to pass through. This wasn't the third room, only the second, how could he have been so stupid, and he had wasted valuable minutes. Moving quickly but quietly he was on his feet, opening the wretched third door which wasn't even locked at all. He closed it behind him and located a smaller door on the left hand wall. He felt round the architrave and there was the key!

Now to open the door and hope that Fern wouldn't scream or shout with surprise. Seconds later he was by the bed. Feeling gently across her face, he discovered she had been gagged. She shook her head and was suddenly awake. She made muffled noises and defiantly strained at the ropes which held her wrists and legs.

'Fern, it's me . . . Jason. Stay quiet and we'll get out alive,' he said before undoing the gag and cutting the bonds.

She rubbed her wrists in the darkness and put her hands out to find his face. When she succeeded she pulled him down on to her mouth and expressed her pleasure as only a hot-blooded woman could.

Both were panting with satisfaction at the long embrace and both secretly wishing there was more time for the intimacy. But the danger was too real and they had yet to make good their escape. He put his finger on her lips so she wouldn't say anything and then leant very close to whisper in her ear about how he hoped to get them back to South Bend, and a bit more besides.

The deep black silence in the house was like a heavy weight that they had to carry with them through the rooms. The ticking clock was their only point of external reference. Moonlight filtered through the shutters, painting short white stripes across the polished floorboards and assisting with avoiding tables, chairs and sundry obstacles.

With hindsight they could have walked perfectly normally through the house, opening and closing doors, as there wasn't the slightest stirring of anything anywhere. At the time it seemed eerily unnatural but once out into the yard with as much haste as could be allowed, they reached Jason's horse, took another for Fern and having led them well away from the bunkhouse, mounted and proceeded to the road-way, breaking into a gallop at the earliest opportunity.

Reining in just shy of South Bend, Jason leant across to Fern and taking her slightly awkwardly in his arms while the horses were so close together, kissed her one more time.

'Don't say anything,' he commanded as they broke free. 'Just go. Just go.'

She looked longingly at him, the red of her hair glinting in the moonlight and the tears in her eyes sparkling like dew. She mustered a smile, turned the horse's head and rode for home. Jason watched her go then caught a piece of dust in his eye which he quickly wiped aside, but the shadows had swallowed her up in that brief moment.

He pressed his heels into his horse and trotted on through the scrub to the west, skirting all tracks into South Bend and coming circuitously to the back of Patty's Place just as the sky was beginning to lighten on the eastern horizon. Slipping silently through the kitchen, he was about to go up the stairs to his room when he was stopped in his tracks.

'Jason?' Riley whispered. 'I'm glad to see you. I was getting worried again, only this time my pa said I wasn't to go looking for you as you could look after yourself. I said if that was the case you'd still be tied up in the ranch out North River way.'

Jason breathed a slight laugh and looked directly at Riley, who was curled up in a big wing chair by the reception desk. 'Have you been sitting there all night?'

'All night,' she repeated. 'I need to

tell you something.'

He shook his head. 'No, not now, I can't keep awake a moment longer, I need a couple hours. You can wake me with some good hot coffee, a side of bacon and some eggs. OK?'

'But it's real important . . . '

He held up an admonishing finger and Riley decided it would be better to obey although it went against her nature.

Jason said again, 'A couple hours won't make any difference.'

He was wrong.

16

Eager to comply with his breakfast request, Riley skipped up the stairs to Jason's room and knocked on the door. There was no reply so she went in. Jason was fast asleep. She touched him lightly on his bare shoulder and his hand dived under his pillow, emerging with a cocked six-gun. Riley fell back with surprise. Jason lowered the firing pin as he hoisted himself up on one elbow. He was bleary eyed and she smiled at him in a tender-hearted way.

'Coffee's ready in the kitchen and I'm just about to cook the eggs.'

Replacing his gun and rubbing his eyes, Jason nodded at her while blinking his eyelids to banish the sleep. He was drained and slumped back on to the pillow. He exhaled a deep sigh then sprung into action and leapt out of the bed. Riley was shocked at the sight and he quickly grabbed a towel to cover his embarrassment.

'Gee, Riley, I'm sorry, I wasn't thinking straight.'

She turned to leave the room but paused by the door. 'Jason, that's a nasty gash in your side,' she said, having seen the livid white scar.

'A flesh wound,' he said. 'A long time ago.' His hand went to his side and he winced involuntarily, not from the touch but suddenly remembering the searing shock of hot lead, now knowing a lot more about how it happened than he did at the time.

Seeing his pain, Riley looked sympathetically at him and wanted to give some comfort but mindful that he had only a towel for covering up, she raised her eyebrows, pouted her mouth and ran the tip of her tongue round her lips.

'Bad boy,' she said and closed the door behind her.

While pouring a second cup of coffee for Jason as he forked his third fried egg on to a thick slice of hot bacon, Riley could contain herself no longer. She had important news to impart.

'Two men came to the hotel yesterday asking after you,' she said casually.

The fork hesitated a moment in mid air before completing its journey to Jason's mouth. He looked at Riley quizzically while chewing.

'They said they were from Blackstone and wanted to speak with you real bad.' Jason was still chewing the bacon. 'They looked like lawmen to me but I didn't see no badges or anything. They weren't the outlaw type like you,' she joked, 'but I didn't like the look of them. Pa spoke with them and they left, but I think they'll be back.'

Just then Cal walked into the kitchen. 'Jason, I'm glad to see you, boy. I think there's going to be some trouble.'

'What's new?' Jason said wryly.

'I mean serious trouble. You're a wanted man by all accounts.'

'Wanted? On what charge?'

'Something to do with a saloon bar brawl down in Blackstone. You killed someone, they said.'

'Like hell I did,' Jason said choking on his food. 'I should've maybe . . . '

'It might be best if you stay out of sight for a while. Soon as you've finished eating I want you to come through to the back parlour, Bern Goodfield said he's got some news to interest you.'

Jason realized there was little time to waste, if Cal was right about the rumour then the sheriff at Blackstone was a dangerously crooked lawman residing in Richer's pocket. He quickly finished his grub and went through to the parlour where Cal was waiting.

'Where's Bern?' Jason asked but didn't wait for an answer. 'Look, Cal, I shot a bummer in the arm after he pulled a gun on me,' he said to allay Cal's worries.

'I don't care about that, Jason, Richer might even be behind that as well, I think he knows something about you. Perhaps it's time you levelled with me. Who exactly are you?'

'I ... I ... ' Jason hesitated, not knowing what to say. 'Listen, I've got all the evidence we need to put Richer behind bars,' he said proudly. 'The railway's coming to South Bend, not North River and Richer's behind all the evictions and burnings. He's the one — '

But Cal held up his hand. 'Yes, yes, we know all about that.'

'You do?'

'Of course. Some of us have known it for ages. Land clearance, cattle yards, cheap land at North River and all that, but nobody believed what they were looking at. Richer is a big noise here and he throws his money around, he forked out half the cost of the church and he pays for the Friday dances, drinks and everything for free. He has friends, spies and agents everywhere. We can't do nothin' about him. There isn't any way of stopping him that we can figure. Since the election meeting, more people are beginning to question his motives, but I haven't got a chance of winning the vote and I guess one day South Bend will become Richton or Richerville or something like. One day he'll end up in the Senate if he isn't stopped.'

Jason frowned. 'Cal, don't mind me sayin' this, but I heard that you agreed to stand against Richer just to make it look like a fair fight, knowing he'd win anyway.'

Cal looked aghast. 'Have you been eating locoweed?'

So Jason told him exactly what had happened since he rode out towards North River with Fern yesterday.

' . . . and that's not all,' Jason said, 'I don't care about the railway, nor all that much about South Bend to tell the truth, it was only chance that brought me here in the first place on the trail of the guilty parties in the Danville stagecoach robbery.'

Cal shook his head. 'Ain't never heard of Danville.'

'No,' said Jason, 'I guess not. It's a town back East and my pa was on his way there on the stage when it was robbed. There was $1,200 in used banknotes and people thought it was just a robbery.'

'But it wasn't?'

'No, sir, it was not, it was cold-blooded murder.'

'Your pa?' Cal asked, his brow knitting furrows to hold Jason's story.

'My pa was a county prosecutor and he was on his way to Danville for the trial of a high profile criminal, Jonathan Poore, with the evidence that would hang him. He didn't know that the jail had been busted the night before.'

'And your pa was killed in the robbery by this man Poore?'

Jason looked away and his eyes were very distant, he breathed a heavy sigh. 'Yes he was. Shot in cold blood. It was more like an execution. There was just the driver, one guard and two passengers on the coach that day. When it approached a particular place which must have been prearranged, the driver reined in and stopped. My pa got out and asked him why, but both the driver and the guard jumped down, took the spare horses and rode off at speed. At the same time three horsemen turned up while my pa was still outside. He stood there with his hands up high while they took the packet of $1,200 from the driver's safe box. They made my pa fetch his trial papers from the coach and hand them over, then they shot him dead and rode off.'

'And so there was no trial and the robbers weren't caught? But what about the other person on the coach? You said there were two passengers.'

'He was hiding under the seat at first but hearing the voices he went out with his hands up.'

'Coward!' said Cal.

'He was only a boy, eight years old, what could he do?'

'That's different,' Cal agreed.

Jason moistened his lips with his tongue. 'I'll tell you what he did. He went and stood in front of his pa so they wouldn't shoot him.'

'That took some guts. But they shot him anyway?'

'Yes, they did. One of them did. Shot him in the back as he grabbed his son round the waist and turned his back on the gunmen. At point blank range the bullet killed him instantly, went straight through his body and stopped halfway through the boy. They both fell to the ground and, covered by his father's body, the boy lost consciousness.'

'But the boy didn't die?'

'No, he didn't. When he came round it was completely silent, silent except for the buzzing of the flies feasting on the fresh blood. He struggled his way free, took a cover out of the coach, leant down and kissed his pa on the forehead and covered the body. He took a horse out of the coach harness and rode back home to raise the alarm.'

'Then . . . '

'Then his ma sat beside his bed for days on end as he lay unconscious, feverishly on the edge of life. When he eventually recovered he remembered nothing of the event. Years later, following in his father's footsteps, he studied law so he could build a decent life for himself and his ma, and carry on his pa's fight against robbers and murderers.'

'We could do with him out here,' said Cal, looking knowingly at Jason. 'Outlaws are two a penny hereabouts. Anyways what was he waiting for, this student of the law?'

'The names. He was waiting for the names, and one in particular, the one who fired the gun.'

'Presumably the man waiting for trial and sprung from jail, Mr Jonathan Poore,' surmised Cal.

'Or one of the other two,' said Jason. 'Linmar and Chambers. Which one was it?'

'And does this boy know yet?' Cal said, riveting Jason squarely in the eye while narrowing his own. 'Does he?' he repeated pointedly.

'He does,' said Jason. 'The Danville stagecoach event wasn't robbery, it was cover for murdering a state prosecutor who was going to ensure Poore was hanged. All three robbers had a life-long taste for stagecoaches and trains, and they carried on robbing for several years until they pulled off the big one near $150,000 which they split. Then Linmar went his own way while the other two stayed together. All three changed their names. Linmar became Marlin and he was hanged in Linken a few days ago. Chambers became Beecham. Those two just more or less turned their names around, but with all that money Poore literally decided to become Richer.'

Cal's eyes widened. 'Nathan Richer! And he was the one who shot your pa?'

'Marlin confirmed it when I saw him a few days ago in jail, and he freely gave a sworn statement to clear his conscience on that crime before I watched him hanged for others. He said Richer thought I was dead too, he thought the bullet had killed us both. All that information's with a marshal back

241

East.' He paused, pleased that at last he'd been able to confide the real purpose of his presence in South Bend.

Jason took a deep breath and exhaled all his pent up anger. Then, more measured, he continued, 'Anyways, Bern Goodfield was trying to dig up some information for me on Richer. I expect that's what he wants to see me about so I'll get over to the newspaper office before making myself scarce.'

'And Beecham is still protecting Richer. Or too scared to leave him. But what are you going to do about them?' Cal asked.

Jason got up and moved towards the door. 'Don't worry, Cal, it's all in hand. I sent a wire from Blackstone.'

Crossing Main Street to the newspaper office with a lightness of step, Jason began to feel at last all his plans were coming together. There was an end in sight and he whistled to the sky because the clouds which had hung over him for so long were beginning to clear. The actual sky at that moment was not so promising. Heavy black clouds were gathering to the west and the sun's rays were still watery in the sharp spring air.

The newspaper office was as noisy as usual with chatter, compositing and clattering machinery. So much so that nobody looked up as Jason entered despite having set off the jangling bell on the door. Bern had his back turned and nearly jumped out of his skin when Jason touched him on the shoulder.

'God save me!' exploded Bern, turning round. 'You near gave me heart failure, Jason.'

Jason watched Bern lick his lips as if they had dried with fright and his eyes darted all over the place. 'Why so jumpy?'

Bern held up his hand to silence him. 'Nothing to do with me, nothing at all, no choice, Jason, no choice.'

'What are you talking about? Did you find me some more information on Richer?'

'I did,' he said, 'but there are two gentlemen who want to tell you something very important about Mr Richer which they say may change your mind.' He avoided eye contact by looking at the floor. 'Come through to the back office . . . ' He led the way and Jason followed. 'They've got a warrant they want you to see . . . '

Bern opened the door, letting Jason go through first. 'I'll join you in a moment.' He closed the door.

There were two men in the room, one sitting behind the desk, the other standing by the back door. Jason had never seen them before. There was a swagger about them he didn't like. The one at the desk was wearing a silver deputy's badge and there was a document laid out. He signalled Jason to take a seat. Jason sat while glancing sideways at the other man who had a jutting, unshaven jaw reminiscent of an ugly bulldog, his thumbs stuck into his gunbelt.

'Mr Colebrook,' said the deputy with an ingratiating smile, 'good of you to see us. I understand you have some interest in Mr Richer. I want you to see this warrant,' he said, pushing it across the desk.

As Jason leant over to take the paper, the second man moved swiftly from the back door and bringing his fist down sharp on the back of Jason's head, slumped him half across the desk and half sliding on to the floor. Jason's eyes rolled and he slipped into a dark and silent world.

Unconsciousness dissipated and Jason emerged from oblivion with a strange sensation of weightlessness. He tried to move as if swimming out of the blurry netherworld but couldn't understand why neither his arms nor legs would move. Soon coming more fully to his senses, he realized he was being carried, trussed and gagged between the two men. They heaved him into the back of a wagon and pulled a heavy tarpaulin over him. Jason's befuddled brain was incapable of fathoming their purpose, but for some reason he was being spirited away, hidden in a cart.

17

Unable to move more than a body roll either way, there was little point in struggling. Instead Jason tried to make some sense of his rather bleak situation. If he was being arrested by a bona fide deputy why the secrecy, and more importantly, where was he being taken? With other senses severely curtailed, Jason's hearing became acute. The horses were being moved very slowly. The cart did a right hand turn, they were going to travel directly into the scrub behind the buildings instead of going down Main Street. By the jolts and jars Jason could tell they were skirting South Bend well away from the main tracks. Then there was a short downhill section and hearing other horses and general road activity, he surmised they were back on the roadway travelling south.

In this unfamiliar and dangerous predicament Jason's wits were sharpened to a point. He wondered first about the badge. One thing was very clear. This was no ordinary arrest. So what was Bern Goodfield's part in it? It was Cal who said that Bern wanted to see him, and it was into Cal's ear that he had just put almost all his evidence. Could Richer have been right about Cal being a friend of his or was it just bluff? If he had put his trust in the wrong people it was too late to worry.

But wait a minute, that couldn't be right. If Bern was in on this, he surely wouldn't have allowed his office to be used for a kidnapping, and Cal would never have agreed to put Jason at any kind of risk, would he? So Bern must know by now that Jason wasn't in the back office, nor were the other two men. Did he suspect nothing? Or were they looking for him right now, had he told Cal Herman what had happened? But as he chewed it over, it just got more puzzling.

It's difficult to figure distances when you're covered with a tarpaulin and thinking about other things. But Jason knew they must surely be getting near the Circle R by now. He expected the cart to slow and turn into the track at any moment. He was going to be brought, tied and gagged before Richer and the warrant which he had provided the evidence for would be put on the table and Richer would ask him what the hell he thought he was doing. Or maybe Beecham was handling all this without telling Richer about the warrant. In which case this could be the end of the road, literally. His situation looked less and less promising and his actions spectacularly ill-judged.

But nothing of the sort happened. He could hear muffled voices of the two men in occasional conversation but indistinct. After another ten or fifteen minutes it became quite clear they couldn't be going to the Circle R.

So where then?

Perhaps they hadn't yet discovered

that he had gone missing from Circle R or it would surely have been Pinero and Pinkie who turned up to look for him. Nor did it seem likely that they were planning to dispose of him in a shallow grave. That would surely have happened by now. What then?

When riding a horse, nobody is aware of the small ruts and occasional stony humps in a road. Back East the well-sprung buggies would barely register more than a slight tilt this way or that. But lying on the hard boards of a small wagon, Jason was beginning to feel every minor indentation and miniscule excrescence as if it was a two-foot ditch or bone-rattling ridge. The journey seemed interminable.

Suddenly the wagon slowed and turned off the road on to a rough track for a short distance before being pulled up. The respite was welcome. In a moment the tarpaulin was lifted and Jason was blinded by the sudden assault of sunlight.

'Short stop for coffee and stretch our

legs,' said the deputy as he pulled Jason into a sitting position, resting against the backboard.

Jason's eyes gradually accustomed to the light as he watched the deputy's assistant making a fire. He was grateful for the chance to move and waggled his head at the deputy in the hope of having the gag removed.

'There ain't no point in shouting or calling out, so make sure you keep your mouth shut,' said the deputy as he loosened the gag.

Jason worked his mouth back into its proper shape while his brain rode rodeo with the possibilities for escape. But there was no hope while his legs were tied together. If only he could get them to release his legs, he might have a sporting chance. But then what? Dodge bullets while running through the scrub and undergrowth with his hands bound together and hope to remain unscathed? If he did manage to get a start wouldn't they just shoot him down?

The sun's rays filtered though the pine-needles catching the patches of fresh grass with bright green daubs. The air was quite still under the trees and the smoke from the fire rose in pretty much a straight line until eddies around the branches put a kink in it. In any other circumstances this would be a pleasant stop, especially as they had rolled Jason a smoke and stuck it in his mouth for him while his conjoined hands held on to the hot tin mug with the delicious bittersweet aroma wafting to his nostrils.

He leant over the side of the cart. 'It sure would be nice to stretch my legs for a moment.'

'Sure it would,' said the deputy's sidekick. 'An' then we gotta chase you through the woods like a jack rabbit when you make a run fer it, an' then shoot you down.' He grinned at Jason through teeth with too much space between them. 'This is goin' to be all legal accordin' to the law, mister. The only thing you're going to have stretched is your neck.'

'That's enough, Gappy,' said the deputy, getting to his feet. 'We'd best be gettin' on now.' He threw the dregs of coffee aside. 'Kick out the fire, Gappy.'

Gappy crossed to Jason and took the mug. Seeing Jason's quizzical look, his eyes narrowed slightly. 'Murder is a hanging offence,' he said without emotion.

'I haven't murdered anyone,' said Jason. Gappy made no reply as he pushed Jason back under the tarpaulin.

The wagon rocked as the two jumped aboard. 'He didn't need to be told that,' said the deputy to Gappy, then, 'git on there,' to the horse and they were back on the road.

The minutes ticked by and Jason began to doze. How could he be on a murder charge, he had deliberately kept himself out of trouble. Well, one or two minor scrapes but nothing like murder. Racking his brain, he drifted in and out of the dark environment which was part tarpaulin and part imagination accentuated by the rumbling axles and lurching motion of the wagon. The minutes turned into hours before sounds of people and horses, wagons and barking dogs brought him back to his deep black reality. The air under the tarpaulin was hot and stuffy. Beads of sweat were stuck to his forehead and the gag seemed to have tightened a couple of notches. Unless he had slept for more hours than he realized, this place was most likely Blackstone.

It was not long before he was carried into the sheriff's office through the back door and into a cell. He was untied and pushed on to the wooden bench which served both as seat and bed. The cell door was slammed and locked. A second iron grid which separated the cells from the office was swung closed and locked, and Jason was left rubbing his wrists and ankles, and stroking his jaw.

'Nice job, boys,' said the sheriff, walking to the grid and looking down the corridor to the cells. He saw Jason nursing his soreness. 'Good to see you again,' he called out sarcastically. 'This is the end of the road for you, Mr Troublemaker. Sure thing, end of the road.'

Jason couldn't restrain his anger. He leapt to his feet somewhat shakily. 'On what charge?'

'What charge?' repeated the sheriff, laughing. 'What charge? Bill Smithers is dead, mister, an' your bullet done him in.'

'It was a flesh wound,' Jason said dismissively. 'I watched the doc patch him up.'

'Well, it didn't do no good. He's dead. Anyways, you have quite a history, I hear. Robbery, kidnapping, bank raids and now murder. Jim Tracey told me all about it. He said you were bragging about all the things you done and now wanted to settle down. Well, you can. When the judge has finished with you, you'll be settlin' down here fer good, just like you wanted.' He laughed again.

Jason was about to say more but realizing it would be pointless, he turned away and sat on the bench.

The sheriff hadn't finished. 'Like I told you the other day, the county judge is due in a couple weeks so make yourself comfortable ... ' He went back into the office. 'Brad, you'd better take that badge off now before anyone here sees it. Go and get Jim Tracey, we need a sworn identification to file with Tracey's deposition sayin' we got the right man. Gappy, ride back to South Bend an' tell Mr Beecham we got him.'

The sheriff's two henchmen left. There was a rattle of coffee can on the stove, 'You want a coffee, Mr Colebrook?'

'Sure,' said Jason, 'have you got any tobacco?'

Out of sight in the office, the sheriff laughed out loud while pouring the coffee. He called out to Jason, 'We don't allow smokin' in the cells, mister.' He unlocked the first door and came towards the cell. 'Feller set his clothes on fire once and managed to get away in the confusion.' He put the tin mug on the floor within reach and stepped back. 'You'll have to think of somethin' better 'an that. But frankly I wouldn't bother wasting your brains on it.'

Before he had finished his coffee, Jason heard the office door open; footsteps and talking drifted through to the cell.

'In here,' said the sheriff, appearing at the grid which he unlocked. He was followed by his badge-toting sidekick Brad leading Jim Tracey.

Tracey came close to the cell and pushed a newspaper through the bars for Jason.

'What's that?' Jason asked.

'It's the newspaper you wouldn't trust me to buy, Mr Colebrook. You see, I'm much more trustworthy than you think. I guessed you might need something to pass the time of day.' He laughed a mean laugh and turned to the sheriff. 'Yes, that's him.'

'How's Abe?' said Jason to Tracey's back.

'Abe? I don't know. He took off yesterday, said he had some business to attend to.'

Jason wasn't sure whether to smile to himself or not, either Abe believed him and got out while he could or he'd been otherwise disposed of. The three of them went back into the office and talked in low voices so that Jason couldn't make out what they were discussing, it was just the tone, the rise and fall which told him crooked dealing was going on. They were all in the pay of Richer, that was certain. Maybe the county judge was, too. Only the train arriving down south in Filmont Junction could bring him any good news. Then the office door opened again and Jason saw the grid being opened and a rather pretty girl carried a tin plate piled high with hot beans to his cell. She handed it to him through the horizontal gap above the lock while the sheriff had a gun trained on him to prevent any funny business.

'At least you won't die of starvation in my jail,' chuckled the sheriff.

Daylight had long since gone, the plate of beans was now empty. The cell was cold and the single blanket thin and scratchy. There was muffled noise from the front office as the sheriff and Brad played a few hands of poker. Light from their oil lamp threw wild, peculiar shadows through the doorway. The riffling of shuffled cards and their light drop on the wooden top of the desk was the last thing Jason heard before his overworked brain gave up the prospect of salvation. He chucked out thoughts of escape like low value spot cards. What he needed was a pair of aces at the very least, but under the circumstances, stretched out on the unforgiving wooden bench, that felt like a very distant hope.

18

Away in the depths of oblivion, Jason didn't yet know that he was in fact holding the much needed metaphorical pair of aces. Back in South Bend there had been a good deal of urgent activity carried out with care and circumspection. Final touches were being put to the bunting and banners which had been decorating the town since the weekend and there was a good deal of hustle and bustle in preparation for the election of the town mayor on Wednesday. Drink had been flowing freely in both the town saloons. Cal Herman had been pouring free beer for his supporters in Patty's Place, and across the street the Two Peaks Saloon had been doing the same for Nathan Richer's followers. It was obvious to the townsfolk which bar was doing the most trade, which was just as well because Patty and Riley had to run around serving their customers as Cal was otherwise occupied.

When Bern Goodfield had eventually gone into the back office, and found nobody there, he was immediately suspicious. Everything had seemed in order with the deputy who had arrived to see Jason. The warrant Bern had been shown for the arrest of Nathan Richer was properly signed and sealed. Before going to the Circle R to serve the warrant, the deputy had simply wanted Jason to confirm the information. Since Jason was due to come across to see Bern he told the deputy and his assistant to wait in the office. So where had they gone with Jason? Had they just left by the back door and ridden off? Surely not, because they wouldn't be taking Jason with them to the Circle R. At least not unless . . .

That's when Bern Goodfield started to wonder what had happened.

Bern opened the back door and looked out. There was no sign of anybody. He took off his green eye-shade and apron and hung them on his office door before going through to the front. He went out to the boardwalk and looked for the two horses. They weren't there. Come to think of it, he hadn't seen any horses hitched up when the deputy and his assistant came into the office. He made a quick decision and walked briskly across to Patty's Place.

'Cal, I might need your help,' he began in a flustered manner, 'no, I *do* need your help. It's about Jason . . . '

'Yes,' said Cal, 'I sent him over a while ago.'

'But he's not there now . . . '

'So? What are you saying, Bern?'

Bern explained about the two men asking after Jason and on hearing this, Cal told him to go back to his office where he would join him in a moment. Then Cal went through to the kitchen hitching on his gunbelt.

'Patty, Riley, look to the bar, I'll be back in a minute.'

He left quietly by the back door, fearing the worst. Arriving at the newspaper office, he immediately searched round the back with Bern.

'They came on two horses?' Cal asked.

'Guess so,' said Bern, pushing his glasses further back on to his nose. 'Leastways, what else?'

'A one-horse cart?' said Cal. 'Look here, no mistake, that's fresh and heading into the scrub. And another horse walking beside it.'

'Do you think they've got Jason?' Bern asked, beginning to feel he had done something very dumb.

Cal looked him in the eye. 'And with a warrant for Richer? They must be taking him to the Circle R. Jesus, Bern, Jason's a goner. How long ago did they leave?'

'Fifteen minutes, twenty at most. What are you going to do?'

'I'll let Geb Nolan decide that. You go back to your work.' He got up quickly from examining the tracks and made all haste to the sheriff's office where he burst through the door.

Geb Nolan was perched on the edge of his desk. Dale was sitting in a chair and looking very worried. Nolan looked up surprised at the sudden clatter.

'Cal!' said the sheriff in cheery greeting.

'Geb! We need a small posse, Jason Colebrook's in grave danger. He's been taken to Circle R with two men posing as deputies or something. My hunch is they're going to hang him.'

Sensing the urgency, the sheriff was on his feet and unlocking the gun cupboard. He tossed a Winchester to Dale. 'Can you shoot straight?'

Dale looked surprised. 'I'll try.'

'Give me another, I'll fetch the Easton boy,' said Cal, 'we need to ride out fast.'

In not much more than the blink of an eye, or two eyes at most, four riders departed South Bend in a noticeable hurry, leaving a few townsfolk with quizzical looks on their faces. Luckily the continuing preparations for tomorrow's election soon erased any concern about the sheriff hurrying out of town.

A little while later, pacing around beside the entrance to the Circle R, Geb Nolan couldn't find any trace of fresh wagon wheels. In fact, there was hardly any evidence of recent movement either in or out of the ranch track. Cal dismounted and poked about as well. Confused, he crossed to the further side of the road.

'Ha! Look here, Geb, these tracks are fresh and those wheels are about the right distance apart. This could be the one. The wagon isn't carrying much of a load, the ruts ain't too deep. They could have stopped here and then walked down the track or something.'

'I don't reckon so,' said the sheriff. 'There'd be no point in that. Why not just ride on down? Why do they want to hang him anyway?'

'He knows too much about what's going on and they must have found out what he's planning.'

'And what's that?'

'He's going to stop Richer becoming mayor.'

The sheriff stopped looking at the tracks and put his hands on his hips. 'Ah, now I see why you want to rescue him.'

'What?' said Cal.

'Look, Cal, I don't know this Jason Colebrook feller too well, and you're about as decent a man as I could ever hope to meet. But I can't take sides in the election. If people see me helping you against Nathan that undermines my authority. I gotta stay impartial. If someone's run off with Jason, I need some firm evidence. Not just this stuff about stopping Richer so you can be mayor. Now you give me some proof he's been taken off against his will and I'll do what I have to . . . '

'Well, I know something that might help,' said Dale slightly nervously, 'that's what I was talking to you about, Sheriff.'

Cal turned to Dale. 'What do you know, son?'

The sheriff intervened. 'Dale was telling me Rosco James and his daughter have left town. Leastways, he hasn't seen them for a couple days and their office has been cleared out.'

Dale suddenly found a bit of confidence. 'Fern told me they'd been holding her at the Circle R, and Jason was there, too, and he got her out and told her to get out of South Bend before it all turned sour. That's what she told me. Said I could go along with them, but I hadn't decided. Now I can't find them.'

'Perhaps they've got Rosco and Fern as well as Jason,' suggested Cal.

'Perhaps,' said Geb, 'but I need evidence, not hunches and hearsay.' He paused and kicked the dirt about with his boot. 'I'm sorry, Cal, I can't go on with this.' He turned to Matt and Dale. 'You two boys decide for yourselves.'

'Do I get to hold on to the gun?' asked Dale.

The sheriff nodded. 'Until you get back to town.'

Matt checked the slugs in his own six gun and looked to Cal. 'I'm with you.'

Dale hesitated. 'I guess I owe Jason. I'll stay with Cal.'

The sheriff mounted up and pulled his horse round toward South Bend. 'Evidence, Cal, bring me something to go on.' He kicked in and rode off.

Cal walked over to Matt and Dale. 'I want to take a look at the Circle R, just to be sure,' he said. 'And thanks for staying with me. Take my horse with you and get yourselves off the track under cover.'

They wandered off as Cal jumped over the railings and went down to the Circle R, skirting the ranch and staying out of sight. Soon he came to the small bluff which overlooked the yard and he settled himself down for some close observation. There were several horses and figures moving about. Nothing appeared urgent or out of place. It didn't feel as if anything was wrong or unusual. Certainly no hanging committee. Time passed, ten minutes, fifteen. He waited and watched. Then some activity began.

Saddles were being checked and cinches buckled. It looked as if half a dozen people were preparing to ride out. There seemed to be a lot of discussing going on. But there was no sign of Jason, no sign of the Jameses, either. Then Nathan Richer came out of the ranch house and mounted up. Another man carrying a banner came across the yard and it dawned on Cal this was just Richer's election party heading into town for him to do some more speech-making at the last moment and sway undecided voters.

When Cal got back to the boys, they stayed under cover and watched for the party to come up the track and turn north towards South Bend. Cal did some puzzling.

'Well, I don't reckon they've got Jason down there, and if he got away from them once they won't give him a second chance. I just hope he's still alive.'

'And I don't think they've got the Jameses,' said Dale. 'I do believe Fern and Mr James moved out and went away. Fern was gatherin' stuff up pretty fast and their wagon was gone, too.'

Cal sighed. 'We got a long ride, boys. The only other place Jason might be is Blackstone. Bern said he thought the deputies were from Blackstone. We have to try. And if he isn't there, then I don't know what.'

They mounted up and turned the horses south towards Blackstone. It was their last hope.

The sun was casting dying rays on the jagged outlines of Blackstone's half-built main street when it finally came into view. The three riders slowed down and turned off the main roadway to skirt round the back of the buildings to glean what they could. Most of the noise was coming from the saloons of course and it spilled out on to the street, filling the cool evening air with a mixture of tuneless music, loud conversation and raucous laughter. Tying their mounts well away under cover, Cal, Matt and Dale staked out the lower end of town near the sheriff's office and jailhouse.

'It's a fair bet if Jason is being held here it would be in a secure place like the jail and my guess would be they're planning to kill him in a fake jailbreak,' suggested Cal.

'Are you so sure someone wants to kill him?' Matt asked.

'I'm sure,' replied Cal, 'he's made a bad mistake in putting his cards on the table too soon and he's the only one who can stop Richer.'

'Richer's the sonofabitch I want to see hanged,' said Matt. 'I'd like to burn him out and leave him dangling in his own barn, just alive enough to know what's happening.'

Cal shook his head. 'Ain't no good feeling like that, Matt. That way you chew yourself up like a dog with a rag.

Jason has a good reason to shoot him in the back, could have done already, but he wouldn't cos he knows that ain't the right way to bring a man to justice.'

'Justice!' exclaimed Matt. 'We're a bit light on that around these parts.'

'You gotta start somewhere, and bit by bit it gets better. This might just be the start for us in South Bend and this whole county. We need more people like Jason Colebrook who live by the law.'

Just then a young woman came over from the saloon opposite with a tray and four steaming plates of food. She went into the sheriff's office.

'He's got to be in there,' said Cal, smiling and showing some emotion for the first time, 'I know it. They got him in there, and we gotta get him out.'

19

Waiting quietly with guns drawn, Cal sent Matt across the street to wait outside the saloon. The sheriff's door opened and the young woman came out. Cal and Dale watched with baited breath as Matt, leaning against a pillar, waited for her to step on to the boardwalk then engage her in conversation. He took her by the arm and whispered in her ear. She laughed and tried to push him off but he didn't let go. He whispered again in her ear and she made some sort of reply while his hands were wandering all over her posterior. She pulled away, slapping his face. He grabbed her and planted a mighty long kiss on her lips; she didn't resist so much and then he let her go. She disappeared through the batwings and Matt wandered back across the street.

'Quite a performance,' said Cal.

'Never mind that,' replied Matt, 'she thinks they've got a prisoner in a cell. The sheriff and one other man are sitting in the front office.'

'But there were four plates on the tray,' said Dale.

'At least Jason's alive,' said Cal.

Matt began to lose his patience. 'If the girl's right, there's two of them and three of us. Let's rush them.'

Cal got up to stretch his legs. 'Dale's got a point. There were four plates so with a plate for Jason there could be three of them, not two.'

'Look,' insisted Matt, 'we've been hanging around long enough, it's time to do something before the saloon starts chucking out the drunks and the brawls begin. I'm going in.'

Cal held him back. 'No, Matt, wait!' He turned to Dale. 'Dale, feeling brave? I want you to go in all casual like, no guns, say you've got a message from Mr Richer. Just say he's coming down himself tomorrow to see Jason

Colebrook. That'll be enough to put them off their guard while we get in behind you. Can you do it?'

Dale licked his lips and sucked in a deep breath. 'Sure,' he said confidently, then added, 'but you best be in quick behind me in case it all goes wrong . . . '

Matt cocked his six-gun and looked at Cal. Cal primed both Winchesters and looked at Dale. Dale climbed the steps to the sheriff's door, opened it, went in and started talking at once in a loud voice. 'Sheriff, I got a message from Mr Richer . . . ' was as far as he got.

Matt almost fell over Dale as he rushed in, pointing the gun square at the sheriff, 'Put 'em up.'

Cal was immediately behind and stuck the barrels of the two Winchesters in the other man's back.

The poker game was brought to an abrupt end as the sheriff and Brad chucked their cards down and raised their hands.

'Sounds good!' said a distant voice, stirring in the cells.

Cal gave a Winchester to Dale to keep Brad covered, then took the keys off the sheriff's desk, unlocked the outer grid and went through to the cells. He opened the cell door, pulled his gun from the holster and handed it to Jason.

'Just in case,' he said. 'We need to get out of here quick.'

Jason told Matt and Dale to sit at the desk and play cards; he rearranged things with the lamp behind them so that anyone casually looking through the window would see only the dark outline of two card players. Jason and Cal secured the sheriff and Brad, and put them bound and gagged in separate cells.

Jason turned to Cal. 'There's another one called Gappy, went off to inform Beecham and he should have got back by now.'

'The fourth plate!' said Cal. 'Beecham went off with Richer into South

Bend to do some electioneering. I saw them all ride out.'

'That explains it,' said Jason. 'Probably had too many drinks, but I wouldn't mind betting they'll be back before too long.'

At that very moment the office door opened and in walked two men. Failing to recognize the two strangers playing cards, they pulled their guns before Matt or Dale had a chance to react. Cal was immediately at the grid with the Winchester aimed at Beecham.

'Take it easy, Beecham,' he said, 'there's four of us and only two of you. Think about it.'

Beecham thought about it and slowly placed his gun on the table while raising his hands, but in that instant Gappy swung round towards the cell corridor and let off a wild shot which struck one of the iron bars by Cal's head, ricocheting into the wall. The whining noise of the bullet disguised another shot in the same moment which blazed out from behind Cal and plugged Gappy full in the chest, smashing right through and throwing him into the office wall. Cal turned round and looked at Jason.

'He had it coming,' said Jason. 'A drunk with a gun can't be saved. His next shot might have done some damage.' He walked over to the desk where Matt and Dale, rather shaken, had dropped their cards. 'Well played!' he joked. 'A winning hand.'

But they didn't laugh.

Beecham was also bound and gagged but not before he sneered at Jason, 'You're an idiot, Colebrook, you can't get away with this, too many people know who you are.'

'And luckily you're not one of them,' said Jason enigmatically.

'We need to get out before anyone comes to investigate the shooting,' said Cal. 'Though I doubt they heard it over the noise from the saloon.'

Jason explained to Cal that he wouldn't be riding back to South Bend with them tonight as he had to go down to Filmont Junction. He retrieved his gunbelt from the sheriff's cabinet and told the others to get going while he had a quiet word with Beecham.

A short blast of cold night air pushed its way past Cal, Matt and Dale as they left the office and skidaddled into the brush to mount up.

Jason went through the iron grid to the cells where Beecham had been tied up in the remaining cell with Jason's empty plate. He loosened the leg-tie enough for movement and eased the gag.

'Sorry I've eaten the beans,' he said. 'If I'd known you were coming down yourself I'd have left you some.'

'You must be mad,' Beecham hissed through the bandana gag. 'There ain't no way you're gettin' out of this alive. You gave us the slip at Circle R with the help of that double-crossing good-fer-nuthin' Colley.'

'He was the only decent one amongst your ragbag of weak-minded sidekicks. People you use for your own ends. Like the crooked sheriff in that cell, or Brad over there in the other cell, and Gappy a dead heap against the wall. All easily swayed from the straight and narrow by a handful of dollars. Pinero and Pinkie, too, most likely. Honest men once, but they never had a chance to live a decent life when they fall in with people like you. You and Nathan Richer, still together after all these years.'

Beecham tried to spit on the floor but the gag reduced his action to a mime, but the words were spat out just as forcefully. 'We're going to string you up right good soon enough, Colebrook. Do you really think you can mess with a man like Richer? A two-bit tinhorn from back East like you? Mister, you've got a lot to learn and not much time to learn it.' He sneered a contemptuous snort. 'You should have been plugged that first day you were poking round Circle R, only we thought to keep you alive to find out who you were.'

Jason smiled. 'And you still don't

know. Sure, Richer's a big man around here all right. So why does he keep you at his side? He needs to keep you quiet, doesn't he, needs to know where you are in case you get greedy and try a bit of blackmail with what you know about Nathan Richer. But then nobody knows who he really is, do they, except you, Mr Hatch Beecham, and it'll soon be time to tell what you know, just to save your own neck.'

Beecham looked at Jason quizzically, his eyes narrowing and his brow furrowing, trying to place the man standing in front of him. But he couldn't find an answer.

Jason smiled at Beecham's confusion. 'Don't worry, I'm not going to leave you here, nor plug you in the back. You're coming with me. Now let's move out.' Jason tightened the gag and pushed him in the back with the barrel of his Colt, steering him towards the door in short shuffling steps.

Outside it was clear and cold, the night sky was cloudless and starry, the

280

noise from the saloon was still boisterous and the few drunks sitting on the opposite boardwalk couldn't focus enough to see what was happening in the dark outside the sheriff's office. Four horses were hitched at the rail. Jason selected one, heaved Beecham across the horse's rump, unhitched it and mounted up.

'Well, Hatch, just like a couple days ago, only I'll be leading this time and you'll be the one who's tied up behind. Funny how things change, isn't it? You see, you're the only remaining witness and I need you alive.'

Beecham grunted, but lying on his stomach straddled across the horse, there wasn't much else he could do.

'How do you fancy a night ride to Filmont Junction? It's a good thing you didn't eat no beans, eh? Riding like that on your belly you'd be puking all the way.'

Jason smiled to himself and pressed his heels into the horse. He leant forward and pulled its ear reassuringly.

'On you go and steady, we've got us a precious cargo and we need him to arrive in good order!'

20

Not surprisingly they passed not one single soul on their way to Filmont in the darkest hours of the night. Riding at a casual walk, out of some consideration for Beecham's uncomfortable position, captor and captive arrived in Filmont Junction in the early hours of the morning. The sun had risen thirty degrees which was enough to bring light to the day but was still taking refuge behind a bank of gathering clouds. The air was damp and rain seemed likely. But the weather was of little interest to Jason. He rode straight to the sheriff's office.

In a busy town like Filmont, the sight of a bounty hunter outside the sheriff's office with a bound victim laid across a horse was not something that aroused more than a passing interest. There were still more than enough ridge riders in these parts to attract young hopefuls looking to make a career out of hunting down outlaws and reaping the irregular rewards. It was a tough life and few of them survived more than a handful of years, sometimes only months or days. Some got enough cash to grab a wife and settle down, some never settled and wandered aimlessly for the rest of their lives, others settled more permanently riddled with bullet holes from a surprise ambush or got outclassed in a gunfight. Too many young men over-estimated their ability and acted the part with loose women and too much liquor. They soon acquired a new home from the undertaker's store of pine boxes.

Depositing his information and telling the sheriff that Beecham would be picked up by tomorrow, Jason saw his captive safely secured in Fremont jail.

'I guess this is the end of the road for you, Mr Chambers,' he said. 'You'll be going back to Danville to stand trial with Mr Poore.'

Beecham looked at him through the bars but wasn't yet fathoming, a furrow began to deepen across his brow and his eyes narrowed, searching for the clue to his captor's identity.

'Not surprising you don't know who I am. My name's not Colebrook. The last time you saw me was twenty years ago. I was just a young boy, eight years old, standing in front of my pa. You know the rest.' He turned and walked away. He heard Beecham calling out to him, but he didn't stop.

Satisfied but churned up inside by unpleasant memories, Jason made his way into one of the many saloons for coffee and breakfast. Chewing on his bacon fat, he couldn't help but feel both pleased and anxious, the job was not yet finished. He swigged some coffee and stared vacantly out of the window at the bustling street. Filmont was more like his own home town than the half-grown settlements of South Bend or Blackstone. For the first time his mind wandered back to Mitchelton and his studies at law school. How different things were out here. Back home shootings and murder were not at all common; most of the time lawyers were arguing over deeds and patents, property and company matters. It all seemed a little dull compared with the last few days!

More than anything else, he wanted his ma to be proud of him and he wondered what she would think, seeing him sitting here like a successful bounty hunter tucking into a well-earned hearty meal. He knew it wouldn't be what she would want of him, but at the same time he felt himself drawn to the thrill of pitting his wits against law-breakers and life-wreckers who masqueraded as honest fellows while trampling across other people's lives and swindling decent folk. Even if he didn't have another reason for bringing Richer to justice, he would be pleased to bring him down for what he was doing to hard-working grafters like the Eastons or Agnes and Barney, cheating his way to other people's hard-earned money. During his court room training, Jason had seen too many people like Richer avoid justice because they could buy a clever lawyer who found a loophole in the semantics of law. How much easier to put a bullet in them or have them strung up by a lynch mob. So long as you have the guilty person, does the process really matter how you deal with them?

Deep in his thoughts, Jason was suddenly brought back to Filmont by the hooting of the early morning train. He got up and headed off to meet some people at the station.

★ ★ ★

Back in South Bend, Main Street was a blaze of colour with bunting criss-crossing the shop fronts passing over the street and back again, zig-zagging all the way from one end to the other. A large banner urged voters to think no further than 'RICHER for Mayor for a

RICHER future' while emblazoned across the front of Patty's Place a painted sheet simply proclaimed 'HER MAN is also YOUR MAN.'

Groups of people stood around discussing anything and everything and wondering what difference would be made by having a mayor. Many were fearful that Richer would simply push more people out of the town and take over everything that's left, making a mockery of years of hard work building the township. But few dared speak out against the most powerful man in the county.

Then the talking stopped and cheers rang out as Richer rode into town with his band of followers to cast their ballot in today's election. Few noticed that the band was a little smaller than yesterday. Nathan Richer, full of swagger, pulled up outside Patty's Place and went through the batwings.

'Good morning, Cal!' he said much too cheerily, offering a hand which Cal reluctantly accepted. 'There's to be no hard feelings one way or the other when they count the votes this afternoon. I am committed to making South Bend into the town it deserves to be.'

'No matter what it takes,' added Cal, wiping out some beer glasses and eyeing Richer carefully. Pinero and Pinkie were close behind him, hovering by the batwings, ensuring that nobody interrupted this chat.

'We can build a prosperous city on these small beginnings, you wait and see, Cal. And I want you to be part of it. Listen, Cal,' said Richer, 'I've lost one of my team. Rosco James has gone missing and I sure would like to find him. Any ideas?' He paused, waiting for Cal to reply but Cal said nothing. 'I was thinking that clever young man Jason Colebrook might like to join my team. You know him pretty well, is he a reliable sort of person? Where could I find him, do you think?'

Cal wanted to say, *You're a foolish, lying sonofabitch, Richer,* but he held his tongue on that one. 'I haven't seen him for a couple days, I heard he'd gone down to Filmont to get the train back East.'

'Ah well,' said Richer, 'no matter.' He headed towards the door but before going out looked over his shoulder, he added, 'Has Hatch been in here already?'

'Not yet this morning,' replied Cal with an inward smile. 'I expect he's got tied up with some business elsewhere.'

The morning continued in anticipated excitement for the townsfolk. The court house had been swept out and the benches polished, a coat of paint had been put on the outside but was taking an age to dry in the cool spring air and signs had been put in place to stop people leaning against the boards. Folk went in and out all morning to put their voting paper in the ballot box under the watchful eye of Sheriff Geb Nolan. The partying started early in the day with Patty's Place and the Two Peaks soon full to busting.

The Circle R crowd were demolishing prime steaks in the Two Peaks, trying to take Richer's mind off two troubling matters and playing down the absence of Rosco James and Hatch Beecham. They couldn't afford to send out search parties when they needed to be seen here in South Bend while people were voting. At Patty's Place, brave souls who dared to be seen siding against Richer were enjoying a hearty beef stew which had been slow cooking overnight and was now served by the steaming bowlful as Patty and Riley ran backwards and forwards to the kitchen to keep the customers satisfied. Cal had to keep opening barrels to stay on top of demand.

At Filmont Junction, Hatch Beecham was poking a fork around his plate of jailhouse mush, protesting his innocence of all and every charge and cursing Jason Colebrook between every unappetizing mouthful. But his protests got no more attention than those of the ragbag of other miscreants being held ready to stand trial before the Cottonwood County judge.

Things were a little different at Blackstone. The town was greatly upset that morning at finding a dead body in the sheriff's office and two men, one of them the sheriff himself, bound and gagged in the cells with no sign of the keys. The blacksmith was fetched to break the locks and get them out. But after that they didn't know what to do. Gappy was fixed up quick with a pine coffin and the grave digger was set to work. They thought about getting up a posse but had too little information to merit rushing around the countryside in the hope of finding something useful. The problem was they didn't know who they were looking for, someone called Jason Colebrook, and the sheriff warned them Colebrook had friends with him and they were too dangerous to take on without a strong posse. It seemed there was nothing to be done. Then suddenly all that changed in a moment.

Six riders came into town, five of them with bright shiny badges. The sixth was Jason Colebrook. The foremost rider pulled up at the sheriff's office while the four deputies behind him pulled Winchesters out of their scabbards.

'Well, folks, I'm US Marshal Ross Klein and I'm taking over this office and arresting anyone here wearing a badge.' He pointed to the sheriff. 'You for a start. Anyone wanting to join him?' The crowd began to shuffle aside. Talk of a posse and other high ideas flew into the wind. The marshal looked at the sheriff. 'I'm placing you under arrest for the misuse of public office.'

Jason dismounted and came forward with a bunch of keys. With one of the deputies, he pulled Brad out of the crowd. 'This one was wearing a badge the other day.' They took him and the sheriff back to the one cell which had its lock intact, secured them and came back into the office.

Marshal Klein turned to the crowd which had grown very quickly as townsfolk rushed over to see what was going on.

'This office is now mine and I'm the

law for the time being. Anyone want to dispute that you'll have a federal judge to answer to, or a piece of hot lead if I prefer. Got it? I'm leaving two deputies here to enforce the law until I get back. Now go about your business.'

Meekly the crowd dispersed, most of the inhabitants quietly pleased that some semblance of law and order might now replace the feeble sheriff and his layabout hangers-on. None of the less law-abiding community in Blackstone was feeling like taking on a US marshal and his gun-trained deputies, and in any case what for? The law was the law and the marshal was the law right now.

The sun was at its zenith and the shadows were at their shortest. The rain had come to nothing more than a sharp shower. After coffee and a smoke and a short rest for the horses Jason, Marshal Klein and the two remaining deputies mounted up and rode out in the direction of South Bend.

21

Voting was over and the South Bend court house was packed to the rafters while the townspeople watched the votes being counted. The ballot box had been emptied on the table and a great mountain of papers sat in front of the two vote counters who represented each candidate — Bern Goodfield for Cal Herman and Zeb Pinero for Nathan Richer. There was only minor disputation about Pinero standing in as a counter for Richer since both his seconders, Rosco James and Hatch Beecham had mysteriously failed to turn up on election day. Sheriff Nolan said it didn't make a heap of difference who did the counting since the whole town was watching so there wouldn't be any cheating. There was little doubt though about who the winner was likely to be as one pile grew faster than the other. The smile of satisfaction on Richer's face grew in line with the number of his votes. He glanced across at Cal.

'Like I said, Cal, there'll be no hard feelings, we can work together on building this town. You and I — '

But he was suddenly interrupted.

'It would be best to stop there,' a voice called out at the court house door.

The room fell silent and a few hundred eyes turned towards the door; people upstairs in the gallery leant over to try and see who had brought the proceedings to a halt.

Jason stepped forward with the marshal close behind while the two deputies stood in the doorway, handguns drawn. 'There isn't going to be any working together with you, Mr Nathan Richer.'

Stepping up to the counting table, Jason said, 'These folk want a mayor who is going to work for the good of the town and its inhabitants. They want a decent, honest and law-abiding citizen like most of these good people in this court house.' He turned to look at the puzzled faces then back to Richer. 'Not someone whose only interest is himself. Someone who'll do anything to get what he wants.'

Then Jason addressed the enthralled audience directly. 'I don't need to look at the pile of ballot papers on the table to know who's going to win. Nor do you, because most of you are too afraid to vote against this man, Mr Nathan Richer. I don't blame you. Anyone who stood in his way got eviction papers and if they didn't go they got run out of town like Barney and Agnes and so many others, or burnt out like the Eastons.'

People began to fidget, they started looking at each other.

Richer was getting angrier by the minute; his eyes started to widen. 'Now look here, Colebrook, I had nothing to do with any of that . . . '

People began murmuring and Jason

raised his voice. 'No, of course not. You send your lackeys like Pinero here.' He pointed to the man at the counting table. 'And Pinkie Yulen, wherever he is.' Jason looked slowly round the room and others started to search with their eyes.

'He's here,' called someone in the gallery.

'Well, hold on to him,' said Jason, 'for his own good.' Then he turned to Richer. 'And perhaps you'd like to tell these good people exactly where the railway is going and why you're building cattle yards on the edge of South Bend.'

'Yes,' called a voice from the body of the room, 'what's going on, Richer?' Then plenty of other voices rose in agreement.

Richer took a step forward and raising his arms to quieten the room, he shook his head. 'Look, folks, things aren't what they seem . . . '

'You're right there,' said Jason, 'and neither are you. Your name isn't Nathan

Richer, same as mine isn't Jason Colebrook.'

Richer turned to face him, but nobody had been watching Pinero slowly slide his hand under the table, quietly slipping his fingers round his gun and easing it out of the holster.

Jason was in full flow. ' . . . your past has at last caught up with you, Mr Jonathan Poore. Twenty years ago you held up the Danville stagecoach to make it look like a robbery, you took the $1,200 from the safe-box, but your motive was to murder my pa, a state prosecutor, who was on his way to your trial with enough evidence to see you hanged for a dozen murders and countless robberies.'

Jason lifted the side of his shirt and showed Richer the livid scar in his side. 'See that? You shot my pa in the back while he was protecting me and we shared the bullet that killed him. Yes, Jonathan Poore, I'm that boy . . . '

There was a sudden commotion by the table and Zeb Pinero leapt to his feet, gun drawn and blasted off two quick shots at Jason. Jason fell to the floor. At the same moment, a piece of hot lead from one of the deputies struck Pinero in the shoulder, throwing him back against the wall, blood spreading across his shirt.

The marshal drew like lightning and trained his gun on Richer. The two deputies had enough of the court house covered and with Sheriff Nolan drawn at the ready on the dais, the atmosphere slowly subsided from tense to edgy and gradually down to calm as Marshal Klein clearly had everything under control. People half out of their seats sat down again, here and there ladies had fainted and were being fanned back to consciousness. Men were standing at the ready, one or two guns had been drawn but no more shots were fired.

With Jason's earlier warning alerting some men in the gallery, Pinkie had been pounced on and was being held motionless on the floor. Cal had rushed across to Jason who had taken both of

Pinero's bullets, one in his chest, the other in his side and had passed out. Riley had leapt up from her seat in the body of the court house and helped her father position Jason more comfortably as he started to come round.

'All right, folks,' said the marshal in a commanding voice, 'the show's over. Let's all go outside nice and quiet, so we can clear up here.'

The crowd made its way quietly to the door and filed outside. As soon as they were in the open, a great clamour of argument broke out as they dispersed in the direction of the two saloons.

'Go and help your mother in the bar,' said Cal to Riley who was reluctant to leave Jason. 'Go on, I'll look after him.'

'No,' she said defiantly, 'you go and do your job pouring beer and let me do mine here.'

Cal hesitated a moment.

'Get along,' said Geb Nolan to him. 'Riley's a big girl now and that's a woman's work.' Cal smiled and went across to Patty's Place.

With the assistance of the two deputies, the marshal took Poore, alias Nathan Richer, and the wounded Pinero to the lock-up. The sheriff supported Jason while Riley gently eased his ripped shirt to look at the wounds. She grimaced at the sight of his torn flesh, quickly applying pressure to stop the bleeding, but there was only one visible wound in his side and a very large red and bruised patch very close to his heart.

'He's going to need the doc,' said Riley, 'it looks like the bullet is still in his side.'

'Can't be,' said Jason through gritted teeth. 'Not at that range. Just stop the blood and get me across to my bed. Then get the doc to stitch me together.'

Dale, concerned about Jason, had been hovering near the door and now seeing his opportunity, he came forward to lend a hand to the sheriff so they could carry Jason to Patty's Place.

They managed to get him on to his

bed with only a couple of minor bumps to his side while coming up the stairs. With great self-control Jason managed not to swear the second time he was bumped against the handrail, but was clearly in agony once lying prostrate on the bed.

'That's as much as we can do,' said the sheriff. 'Dale, go and find the doc, he's probably looking at Pinero's smashed shoulder.'

Dale and the sheriff both left and Riley sat on the edge of the bed. Jason's eyes were closed and his brow was furrowed with the pain. Riley stroked his forehead tenderly.

'Well, Mr Colebrook, or whoever you are, you sure know how to turn a town upside down.' And under her breath to herself, 'And a girl's heart.'

★   ★   ★

It was well into the following morning before Jason began to stir. The first thing he felt was a severe tightness across his chest as if he was bound with ropes. Then he was aware of a gentle rhythmic tapping noise and gradually he emerged from a dreamless sleep. His hand went to his side and feeling first the bandages then the tenderness, things began to fall into place as his eyelids flickered into the daylight. The window was slightly open, the curtain tapping against the frame and the daily buzz of human activity drifted in. Slowly he turned his head sideways and his pupils dilated at the sudden shock of seeing Riley slumped in a chair. Wisps of blonde hair fell across her face, her mouth was slightly open and her breathing deep and regular. She was fast asleep.

Or so he thought. Suddenly she was awake and getting up out of the chair.

'How d'you feel?' she asked. 'The doc said you're a lucky man, two inches shorter and you'd have lost a lung. Not to mention the hole through your heart.'

'That's an odd way of putting it.'

'But you're gonna need a couple weeks of rest.'

'Coffee would be good,' he said.

She smiled and left the room.

Jason woke again and saw Riley sitting in the chair. 'Where's that coffee?' he said.

'Ha,' she laughed. 'Mr Sleepyhead, that was two days ago.'

'What!' he said, trying to sit up.

She gently pushed him back down. 'Relax, Jason. You're mending real good. The doc said another couple days and you can get up.'

'I'm starving.'

'Well, if you can stay awake I'll bring you some steak and eggs. Now lie still, you don't want those stitches coming out yet. And look at this. I found it in your shirt pocket.' She handed him a flattened piece of lead.

'A bullet?' Jason said. 'In my shirt pocket?'

'Along with this.' Riley handed him a very misshapen silver dollar.

Jason rolled it round in his hand.

'God bless that little old lady,' he said under his breath. 'Never refuse a gift.' He looked at the big bruise a little to the left of his heart before sliding back under the covers.

Two days later, glad at last to be up and about again, Jason went down to the kitchen for his breakfast. Riley took him through to the dining room where Matt Easton was sitting at a table with his ma and pa, no longer needing to be in hiding. Ma Easton poured a cup of steaming coffee for him and they all ate breakfast together. Before they had finished Cal came through from the bar.

'It's good to see you've mended, Jason.'

'Where's the marshal?'

'He left the day after the counting. Took Richer with him. Pinero's still here in jail in a bad way.'

'And Pinkie?'

Matt answered, 'He made a run for it.'

'And . . . ' said Jason, wondering.

'Disappeared,' said Matt. 'Half a dozen of us searched around for a couple hours but we lost him.'

Jason shrugged. 'Probably for the best. He'll cause bother wherever he goes and get slugged for his trouble one day. Well, I guess the marshal and his deputies have got Richer and Beecham back East by now. Richer won't avoid getting his neck stretched this time. And I must get back to see my ma.'

Cal put his hand on Jason's shoulder. 'Can we have a chat when you've finished eating? Come through to the bar when you're ready.'

'Sure thing,' said Jason, helping himself to another piece of bacon.

When he had finished he went into the saloon. Cal was cleaning glasses behind the bar. He indicated for Jason to take a seat. 'I've got a couple buddies coming over to join us.'

The batwings opened and Bern Goodfield pushed through, his hands raised in a gesture of complete contrition. 'Jason, I'm so . . . '

'Water under the bridge,' said Jason, 'forget it.'

He was soon followed by Sheriff Nolan, then Joseph McCleery, the town's only remaining lawyer and land agent since the hasty departure of Rosco James. Then came the pastor and two more men Jason didn't know. Quick introductions were made before Cal joined them at the table with a tray of drinks. Before anything else was said they all took a glass, raised it to Jason and drank his good health. Jason's hand darted to his side and pressed it gently.

'Soon, gentlemen, soon,' he said.

'Now see here, Jason,' began Cal. 'While you've been taking a nap upstairs things have moved on here. I now find myself the Mayor of South Bend by common consent. So I've brought together these fine gentlemen here and formed a new town council. We decided we wanted to give you a reward.'

'I've got my reward,' said Jason, 'Richer will face the music and the ultimate penalty of the law, that's why I came here, for the sole purpose of bringing him to justice.'

'But in the meantime,' said Bern Goodfield, 'you saved us all from a swindling crook.' He leant across to Jason and said more quietly, 'Incidentally, could we negotiate exclusive rights to your story?'

They all laughed. Cal continued, 'Marshal Klein said Blackstone will need a new sheriff and he thought you might like the job. He wired to say the people down there are willing to give you a go.'

'That's mighty fine of him,' said Jason, 'but I want to practise law in a court back East, not out here in the West where a gun demands more respect than a court.'

Cal, sucked in, said, 'Well, it's your life of course, Jason. But look, Richer's properties have been confiscated to the town and we want to give you one of the ranches so you can settle down here if you want to. And I know someone who'd really like it if you did.'

There was a pause, then Cal nodded to McCleery.

McCleery pushed a document across the table. 'This has been drawn up according to all the legal requirements, Jason. The ranch out on the North River road, which I believe you've seen, is now in your name, lock, stock and barrel. You're now a land owner in the neighbourhood.' They banged the table with their glasses and clapped, bidding him welcome to Cottonwood County and the township of South Bend. Then silence.

Jason avoided their eyes and fiddled with his glass, pushing it left and right in a paroxysm of indecision. At last he found his voice. 'I don't know what to say. I haven't done enough to deserve this. I appreciate your generosity and I gratefully accept this gift of the ranch. But the cattle there is the herd belonging to the Eastons.'

'Don't worry about that, they're going to rebuild on their own land beyond the railway just as soon as the lumber is ready,' said Cal.

Jason looked round the table at the expectant faces. 'I'm torn, gentlemen . . . friends . . . torn. I don't know if my ma would be willing to move out here, she's kinda settled and has built her life in Mitchelton. I don't know if she would . . . I just don't know . . . and besides . . . '

McCleery came to Jason's aid. 'Listen Jason, there's no need to decide hastily, but now we know the railway is definitely coming to South Bend, this town is going to grow as big as Filmont and we'll need good lawyers to handle the business. It'll be far too much for me on my own. Plenty of room for you to set up, too, Give it some thought.'

The gathering broke up and the newly-formed town council left the saloon. Jason was left alone at the table twisting an empty glass. Cal poured himself a beer and leant on the bar.

'Twenty-eight?' Cal said. 'I met Patty when I was twenty-eight, same as you, she was just twenty and the liveliest girl I'd ever seen. There was a fire in her that lit a spark in me cos she was defiant, oh yes, a real firebrand. A real challenge. Same as Riley, she gets it from her ma. A girl who knows her own mind. I'd never have been so successful without Patty behind me ready to push, make me take a risk. Helped me build this business. Now look at me. Mayor for chrissakes! And standing here with a prosperous hotel in a town that's about to boom.'

Jason took a swig of beer and smacked his lips, deep in thought.

Cal continued. 'You remember the first time you stepped into my bar and spat out that drink?'

'I do.'

'I called you son and you didn't like it. Well, think on it some more. Son-in-law has a kinda nice ring to it, if you see what I mean.'

Jason looked up at Cal leaning on the bar and just caught sight of Riley hovering awkwardly by the door. She didn't want to disturb their conversation and turned back into the hotel.

'Miss!' Jason called out playfully. 'I could sure kill a cup of coffee.'

We do hope that you have enjoyed reading this large print book.

Did you know that all of our titles are available for purchase?

We publish a wide range of high quality large print books including:
Romances, Mysteries, Classics
General Fiction
Non Fiction and Westerns

Special interest titles available in large print are:
The Little Oxford Dictionary
Music Book, Song Book
Hymn Book, Service Book

Also available from us courtesy of Oxford University Press:
Young Readers' Dictionary
(large print edition)
Young Readers' Thesaurus
(large print edition)

For further information or a free brochure, please contact us at:
Ulverscroft Large Print Books Ltd.,
The Green, Bradgate Road, Anstey,
Leicester, LE7 7FU, England.
Tel: (00 44) **0116 236 4325**
Fax: (00 44) **0116 234 0205**